DESERT JUSTICE

DESERT JUSTICE
A SONNY TABOR QUARTET

Paul S. Powers

edited by

Laurie Powers

W

Five Star • Waterville, Maine

First Edition
First Printing: October 2005

Published in 2005 in conjunction with
Golden West Literary Agency.

Set in 11 pt. Plantin by Minnie B. Raven.

Printed in the United States on permanent paper.

Library of Congress Cataloging-in-Publication Data

Powers, Paul S. (Paul Sylvester), 1905–1971.
    Desert justice : a Sonny Tabor quartet / by Paul S. Powers ; edited by Laurie Powers.—1st ed.
        p. cm.
        ISBN 1-59414-154-1 (hc : alk. paper)
        1. Outlaws—Fiction.   2. Western stories.
    I. Powers, Laurie, 1957–   II. Title.
    PS3531.O9725D47 2005
    813′.52—dc22   2005016255

DESERT JUSTICE

TABLE OF CONTENTS

Foreword

Laurie Powers

In the spring of 1929, a young man from Kansas with a head full of stories walked into the lobby of the Willard Hotel in Tucson, Arizona. The place was, as he called it, "the horsiest and by far the cowiest hotel in Pima County," full of ranchers, rodeo riders, and drifters. It was exactly what Paul Powers had been looking for, so he planted his typewriter in a corner of the lobby and went to work. Here was the rich history that he needed for inspiration. It worked, too. That summer a novelette titled "The Eleventh Notch" was published in Street & Smith's *Wild West Weekly* about a young outlaw named Sonny Tabor. One of the most popular characters in the long-running pulp magazine, Sonny was featured in stories that, over the next fifteen years, would be regularly illustrated on the cover of the magazine, spun off into a book, and even adapted into eighteen radio scripts.

In that first story he was an outlaw accused of a string of murders, feared for his accuracy with a gun, and pursued for an extravagant reward of $6,500 for his capture. But to the readers of *Wild West Weekly*, Sonny was a wrongfully accused young man, forced into a life of continual flight who used his guns only in self-defense or to rid the West of unsavory characters. He was always cheerful, optimistic, quick with a gun, and had an incredible work ethic.

Sonny was in many ways typical of many Western pulp fiction heroes during the first part of the 20th Century. And there were plenty of them. Over the twenty-five year period from 1920 to 1945, at least 162 different Western magazines hit the newsstands at one point or another. At one point in 1940, there were thirty-six pulp Western magazines for sale. Much of this popularity can be attributed to the fact that the Great Depression was considered the Golden Age for the Western. Americans could not get over their love affair with the Wild West, despite the fact that the frontier was declared "closed" in 1890. Millions of people still packed up and moved West, hoping to find the life that the West always seemed to promise. Those that didn't move went to the picture show, paid 25¢, and watched reel after reel of "B" Westerns—many of which were spin-offs from pulp Western stories—that starred a cavalcade of cowboy stars. And millions more paid 10¢ for 114 pages of a pulp magazine with no ambiguity in the stories and where the good guy always won.

Once readers read a pulp magazine, they passed it around to other friends. Each issue was, as Sonny's creator wrote, "literally read to pieces." Reader after reader escaped into a world where, at least for a few hours, they could live on a big ranch rather than the stifling apartment in the city. They could look out over a cliff at magnificent landscapes, breathe the clean air, tame that wild bronco, and eat a five-course breakfast. They could derive satisfaction from storylines that meted out appropriate judgment to characters that could always be counted on to have the same characteristics. Bankers were greedy and corrupt, town officials were not to be trusted, lawmen were inept, and those who reeked of bad breeding were murderous and amoral. A common theme in the pulp Western is the downfall of a greedy rancher who bilks poor farmers out of their land—but they always receive their due in the end. Reading a pulp Western story allowed the reader to pretend, at least temporarily, that society's problems could be solved with a swing of a saloon door.

"The Eleventh Notch" was the beginning of the fifteen-year Sonny Tabor saga. But Sonny Tabor was just one of several heroes that Paul Powers created for *Wild West Weekly* from 1928 to the magazine's end in 1943. Kid Wolf, Freckles Malone, Johnny Forty-Five, King Kolt, and the Fightin' Three of the Rockin' T continually appeared in the magazine. Kid Wolf and Sonny Tabor were, as Redd Boggs wrote in *The Pulp Western* (Borgo Press, 1983), "by all odds the favorite characters of nearly all 3W readers, and they continued to appear with scarcely diminished popularity until the very end."

When Paul took up residence in Tucson, he was twenty-four and had already sold twenty-five stories to *Wild West Weekly* over the previous five and a half months, spinning out stories published under at least nine pseudonyms. He had started writing when he was fifteen and sold his first pulp story when he was twenty. But his launch into pulp writing wasn't as effortless as it might seem.

His life was almost as big as those of his heroes, mainly due to his restless and adventurous nature that put him in hot water more than once. By the time he was fifteen, he was wandering away from the Kansas homestead whenever he felt like it, traveling to Denver and Boulder and nearby ghost towns, probably looking for booze, female action, and anything to fill the hole that he would carry within him his entire life. He had accidentally shot himself in the chest practicing gun-slinging techniques, dropped out of high school, and lied about his age and joined the Navy, only to be sent home. There was some jail time in there some-where, the details of which Paul decided to omit from his

11

memoirs, but it probably had something to do with bootleg-
ging.

As a pulp writer, Paul lived a life not unlike Sonny
Tabor. He continually roamed the Southwest with his wife
and children throughout the Depression era. Always
seeking new land to revive his tiring creativity and soothe
his restlessness, he moved his family no less than nineteen
times during the fourteen years he wrote for *Wild West
Weekly*: from Arizona to California, back to various spots in
Arizona, back to California, to New Mexico, and then up
and down the coast of southern California. During that
time Paul would type an average of 12,000 to 15,000 words
of fiction every week, alternating with 5000-word short stories. But it was never enough for the editors of *Wild West
Weekly*, who continually hounded him for his lateness and
his propensity for disappearing for weeks at a time.

Paul Powers was my grandfather, but that was about all I
knew about him. He was an enigma, whose life was a mystery to me until I stumbled upon his career as a pulp writer.
His eldest son, my father, died in 1964 when I was seven
and Paul died in 1971 at the age of sixty-six. When my
grandfather died, it was as if that entire side of the family
died with him. We lost track of my father's half-brother
Tom and sister Pat. As that side of the family drifted away,
so did my grandfather's history as a pulp fiction writer. I
only knew that he had published a Western novel, *Doc
Dillahay* (Macmillan, 1949), and a few small books that I
mistakenly thought were called "dime store novels". I had a
copy of one titled *Spook Riders on the Overland*. It was a
shape and size I had never seen before. It was a small
square book that fit into the palm of my hand, with large
print and crude black and white illustrations. And that was
that.

Then, in 1999, I decided to write a paper on *Doc Dillahay* for an American Studies class while attending Smith College. But I was worried about whether I could find a copy of the book: I had never seen a copy for sale at any used book or antique store, and the only copy I had was stored away in California. But now there was the Internet, and I thought, maybe, just maybe, there would be another copy somewhere. I entered the title *Doc Dillahay* into a nationwide library database. Up popped 75 libraries across the country that had the book. It was in the library at Oxford. It was even published in Braille. I then entered the title *Spook Riders on the Overland*. There it was, Ward Stevens listed as author, and noted as a Big Little Book. I entered the name Ward Stevens and found a half dozen more Big Little Books. One was called *Buckskin and Bullets, A Sonny Tabor Story*. Sonny Tabor? The name Sonny Tabor produced an odd but very exciting find. Eighteen "Sonny Tabor" radio scripts are archived in the Street & Smith collection at Syracuse University, but no other information such as the dates of the scripts or the authors was listed.

After some quick research, I learned that Street & Smith was the most successful publisher of pulp fiction in America for almost a century, beginning in the mid 19th Century and ending in 1950. Could it be that my grandfather wrote pulp fiction stories, also? I called Syracuse. Did they have any record of my grandfather's writing for Street & Smith? They had a few accounting records, they answered, and could forward to me copies of "receipts" showing payment for stories bought by the magazine. I expected to get five, maybe ten, of these receipts. When they arrived, there were eighty for the period between the end of 1939 and 1943. The average word count was 12,000 words per story, all of them sold to *Wild West Weekly*.

For me, a struggling writer who hadn't published so much as one short story, this was almost too much to comprehend. Yet I felt that this wasn't the end of the search. I drove to Syracuse and spent three days in their Special Collections. Cart after cart of bound *Wild West Weekly*s were rolled out for me to investigate. I opened the first one. Sonny Tabor was on the cover. I opened volume after volume; cover after cover featured Sonny Tabor, Kid Wolf, or Freckles Malone. I spent the first day just trying to get a count of how many stories he had written for *Wild West Weekly* and finally gave up because it probably would have taken a week. Eventually I learned the official count: 431.

The town of Little River sits almost precisely in the middle of the state of Kansas, a mid-point between those two infamous cattle outposts of Abilene and Dodge City. But while these towns were famous for barroom brawls and gunfights in the streets, Little River was a sturdy little hamlet growing quietly and peacefully, sponsored by tough farmers and their wives who bore their Midwestern burdens with tolerance and determination. Hard work was the quickest way to find grace with God; dancing and card playing were the quickest way to lose it. There was always activity. The downtown quickly thrived and grew to over twenty businesses by the turn of the century. Picnics by the river were popular on Sundays after church. Little River was still small and isolated, dozens of miles from anything that could be considered substantial civilization. Even with its growing commerce, downtown was not much other than a short row of stores with awnings to shade townsfolk from the brutal Midwest summers, wooden sidewalks and hitching posts to tie up the horse and buggy, and, just past city limits, the endless Kansas plains stretching to the horizon. Wichita, the closest city, was eighty miles away.

Paul Sylvester Powers was born there in 1905, the first-born son of Dr. John Harold Powers and his wife Grace. John was of local stock, growing up in nearby Canton, Kansas, and starting out as a schoolteacher before deciding to become a doctor. After attending medical school in Kansas City, he set up practice in Mitchell, Kansas, and after a few years opened up an office in Little River. He was quite busy; he was the only surgeon in town for quite some time, and spent most of his days away on house calls. Faithfully showing up at farmers' homes with his kind and patient demeanor, Dr. Powers delivered many a baby in the Little River community. Two years after Paul was born, a sister, Nell, arrived.

Paul's mother, Grace, a stately young woman with billowing dark hair, loved the arts and literature and played the mandolin. Her untimely death at the age of thirty from uterine cancer left Paul, at the age of eight, without a mother and "the greatest teacher I'd ever have."

One year after Grace died, John re-married a nurse, Edith Brooks. Edith was a nurse, not a mandolin player or an artist, and, while she was supportive of Paul and pasted his schoolwork on the kitchen wall, she wasn't his mother. In 1915, when Paul was ten, his stepmother gave birth to a daughter, Phyllis, and four years later George was born. The house was quite full now with four children, and, with most of the family attention devoted to the two young babies, Paul began to look for other ways to entertain himself.

He found literature, traveling, and adventure guaranteed remedies for small-town boredom, the classroom, and parental pressures. But even though his house had one of the largest book collections in town—some 300 volumes—they were mainly his father's medical books. Paul felt "starved"

15

for books. Little River had no library. Books, according to Paul, were considered by most of the townsfolk to be "impractical foolishness."

The serious young boy knocked on neighbors' doors and asked if they had any books he could read. There probably wasn't more than "a few wheelbarrows of books in the settlement," Paul complained. Kindly neighbors gave him books to read, but they started to view the little boy, as young as he was, as eccentric and "something of a screwball." Bored and lonely, he escaped into any book he could find. He loved the melodrama of *Les Miserables*, the raw adventure of Jack London, and, of course, was a loyal follower of Frank Merrill, the most popular hero of the American phenomenon known as the pulp magazine.

Pulp fiction magazines, named after the cheap pulp paper on which the pages of the magazines were printed, had their origins in the 19th Century. They were a hybrid of two forms of popular reading: the dime novel, an immensely popular form that surfaced at the time of the Civil War, and "two-penny" publications that featured wildly implausible adventure stories. In 1896, Frank Munsey, publisher of the boys' magazine, *The Argosy*, came up with an idea. He knew that many of his readers wanted to read good stories, but they could not afford the expensive slick magazines that were usually the only source of fiction. He decided to change the entire format of the magazine by omitting any illustrations other than those on the cover. By doing so, he found that he could print a good deal of fiction in one issue and, because he used cheap pulp paper, would only have to charge 10¢. *The Argosy* debuted with its new look and was an immediate success. Pulp magazines eventually dominated the mass fiction market, and dime novels had completely faded away by the 1920s.

By the time Paul was in his first year of high school, he was earning wages as a writer, although he wasn't paid in cash and it was a somewhat illicit undertaking. For the rate of one pack of cigarettes per thousand words, he composed papers for a classmate named Horace who was more adept at football than English. This was respectable compensation, considering that cigarettes were illegal in Kansas at this time. Then Horace approached him with a new assignment—three book reviews were due. Paul was no dummy. He immediately increased his rate for this assignment to four packs.

One day he went to the home of a friend who showed him a correspondence course he was taking. It promised that the student would make bundles of money as a screenplay author. Paul was entranced by the copies of checks and testimonials. After looking at his friend's feeble attempts at scene writing, he knew he could do better. He left a different boy. Why couldn't he make money at this? He had been doing some writing in his notebooks at school for years, and others were paying him to write for him—sort of. "Why couldn't I write some stories? In a small ad in some cheap magazine I was reminded that Jack London received $1,300 for just one short one. An evening's work!" Thus Paul began his writing career, lured by copies of checks.

He scoured magazines and newspapers for potential markets. Magazine articles, journalism, poetry, any type of writing would do. He discovered many newspapers were looking for joke writers who would write two or three liners used as fillers. "I can do that," he recalled, and started to pen two-line jokes, sending them off to places like *The Saturday Evening Post* and the Chicago *Daily News*. At first, they were all returned. Then one day he received a check in the amount of $3.50 from the *Daily News*. Paul was euphoric: "I've received remittances since that were more than a hundred times as large, but none as electrifying as this one. I didn't realize it then, but I had sold my soul into bondage at that moment, sold it to a broadly smiling, very pleasant devil. Bless his heart!"

It fueled him to write more, selling to the *Daily News*, the *Post*, and, later, exclusively to a humor periodical, the *Laugh Factory*. Eventually he was making $25 a week, a princely sum at the time, and enough so that he felt justified in dropping out of school to write full time. At the same time, he wrote short stories and shipped them off to various publications. One of the markets he zoned in on was Street & Smith.

Of the hundreds of publishers that spewed the countless titles of pulp fiction in the first half of the 20th Century, Street & Smith sold hundreds of periodicals, dime novels, and book series with popular titles like the Nick Carter series, *The Yellow Kid*, *The Shadow*, *Doc Savage*, *Detective Story Magazine*, and *Western Story Magazine*, covering genres such as sea adventure, college, detective, federal undercover agents, aviation, movies, romance, romantic Westerns, fame and fortune, among others. In the 1920s, pulp fiction was an enormous market, and Street & Smith was king of the pulp fiction world.

Street & Smith had begun rather modestly in 1855 when Francis Scott Street joined with Francis Shubael Smith and bought the *New York Sunday Dispatch*, a fairly successful Sunday periodical. They had their first huge hit in 1886 with the Nick Carter series. By the 1890s they had successfully launched such series as the *Tip-Top Weekly*, the Frank Merriwell series, and taken over the most popular Western series of the 19th Century, the Buffalo Bill stories. Paul narrowed his focus to *Wild West Weekly*, a magazine that had originated as a Frank Tousey publication in 1902. The format of the magazine had originally been fairly straight-forward, with just one lead character, Young Wild West, a younger mutant of Buffalo Bill. Plenty of heroes with long hair and elegant, fringed buckskin coats already packed the newsstands, however, and the magazine struggled to survive. By the early 1920s, sales had deteriorated to the point that, in order to cut costs, the publisher re-issued earlier stories in new issues. Street & Smith bought *Wild West Weekly* from Tousey and re-launched the magazine in 1927. Young Wild West was still the dominant character, but the magazine altered the format and introduced other Western heroes to boost sales.

From the age of thirteen, Paul hopped between Kansas and Colorado, sometimes with his family, many times by himself. By the time he was nineteen, he had made several trips to Denver and the mining districts of Blackhawk and Central City in mile-high Gilpin County. Both towns, on the western side of Denver, were part of the first mining settlement in Colorado in the 1850s. The area was rich with gold and ore, and Central City quickly became a bustling town, and at one point was bigger than Denver. Blackhawk complemented the industry with smelters to process the minerals. During the latter part of the 19th Century, the area was teeming with prospectors, entrepreneurs, prostitutes, and assorted families attempting to carve a civilized life out of a mining town. But by the time Paul arrived in the late 1910s, both towns were a shadow of what they had once been. Store fronts, staggered on hillsides, were from a glorious bygone era—saloons, hotels, dry goods, clothiers, bakeries. But most of the population had left years before, deserting their homes and mine shafts and leaving empty buildings and an area totally stripped of minerals, trees, and life.

Paul took advantage of the hundreds of abandoned homes and crumbling mine shafts and started to explore. He scrambled around shafts with names such as Fourth of July, Grand Central, Freedom, Climax, and Pocahontas. He pretended to be a mountain man, carrying his Winchester rifle and shooting rabbits for dinner. He walked through dozens of abandoned houses perched on the many hillsides surrounding the towns, scavenging for old furniture and artifacts, such as old letters or documents from the mining period. He also met a young girl who was as vivacious as he was quiet; the attraction was immediate, and Paul and Velma Niccum eloped. They moved back to Little River shortly thereafter, Paul determined to be a writer and Velma pregnant with their first child.

Joke writing eventually started to wane. Paul had to resort to going to work—literally—at the salt mines adjacent to town. He probably only spent a few months there, but the working conditions left a lifelong impression. Twenty years later he still vividly remembered working in the mines and the men that toiled for a lifetime, never able to better their conditions: "These and similar horrors decided me that I would escape, that I would use what brains the gods had given me and become a writer. I felt pity for those unable to escape—who didn't try. Although there is nothing degrading in unskilled labor, I thought, and still do think, that there is plenty of room for improvement in the laborer's standard of living and dying. What could I do, I wondered, to help them out? Well, I could lighten the troubles of some of them, perhaps, by giving them entertainment. The pulp magazines filled a need, for these people didn't buy books."

On November 5, 1924, Paul received a letter. *Weird Tales*, a new pulp that specialized in horror and fantasy stories, was buying his horror story, "The Death Cure". *Weird Tales* had only been in existence for a year or so at this point and was struggling to survive, but eventually it became the most famous and most anthologized pulp magazine in history, partly due to the fact that they made it a habit of buying stories from then-unknown writers like Tennessee Williams, Robert E. Howard, H.P. Lovecraft, and Robert Bloch. They paid Paul $21.75 for the story and published it in 1925. Paul rejoiced "like a man demented," but the rest of the family was only mildly interested. "Everyone seemed to keep their emotions in check," he noted.

Getting that one story published was all he needed. He diligently wrote more stories and sent them off, and promptly quit the salt mines. But it would be a long three years, during which time he would move back to Colorado, then return to Kansas and get divorced, before he would get a steady paycheck. He concentrated on writing Western tales, especially those that were drawn from his experiences climbing through the ghost mining towns of Colorado.

Then, in August 1928, he received a notice from Ronald Oliphant, editor of *Wild West Weekly*:

I am sorry to have to return "The Silver Looters". This is a modern mining camp story and does not quite fit in with the policy of Wild West Weekly which aims in its stories to reproduce the spirit of the really wild West before the introduction of modern machinery and automobiles, *et cetera*.

Paul's heart sank, but the letter continued:

I was pleased to purchase "The Whispering Gunman". This is just about our type of yarn.

21

He was paid $30—a penny a word.

It didn't take long for Oliphant to see that Paul was an industrious worker. Less than two weeks after Paul sold his first story to *Wild West Weekly*, Oliphant suggested that he write more stories for the magazine. They had an open market for not only short stories, but short novels, too. By the end of August, he had already purchased several stories from Paul. He also began to train Paul in the stringent guidelines that dictated pulp Western story lines and character development:

> Do be careful with the ethics of your stories. Do not have the hero lie, swear, drink, steal, or take unfair advantage. Always let him give the other fellow the breaks and then win out.

It made a better story for the hero to get himself out of trouble, instead of being rescued by someone else. Lawmen were never corrupt, only somewhat clueless. Gunfights and fistfights were a necessity for every story, yet the words "blood" and "bleed" were not permitted.

That winter was extremely productive. His second story, "The Gunman of Monterey", introduced Kid Wolf, who, along with Sonny Tabor, became one of *Wild West Weekly*'s most popular characters. Kid Wolf was a renegade, a self-employed independently wealthy rancher from the Río Lobo. Kid wore a fringed buckskin outfit, spoke with a heavy Texas drawl, and rode a magnificent snowy-white steed named Blizzard. At first, Oliphant wasn't keen on the idea of making Kid Wolf a regular; he had too many "Kids" in the magazine as it was. But readers clamored for more, and Paul had his first regular character.

By early 1929, twenty-four-year-old Paul was already a

father (a son, John, named after his father, was born in 1925), divorced, and entrenched in *Wild West Weekly*'s stable of writers. "Now that I was a professional writer of Westerns, I began to realize that there was much about Western life I didn't know, much that I couldn't get by reading. I was fairly familiar with miners and mining, but the Prince of the Western tale was, and will continue to be, the cowboy. Although his environment was rapidly changing, he wasn't yet extinct, and I made up my mind to look him up." That spring Paul packed up his touring Cadillac and moved to Tucson.

"The Eleventh Notch" begins with rancher Ed Stewart discovering the gravesite of his son Robert. A calling card was left—a small note stuffed into a shell cartridge that names Sonny Tabor as the killer. "No. 11" supposedly marks the 11th murder for which Sonny claims credit. Stewart's crew shrinks in fear upon learning that Sonny is the culprit; he's known as the most fearsome killer in the Southwest. But Ed is now out for vengeance, and plans an ambush. Sonny is a "young *hombre*" perpetually nineteen with a youthful face and frank blue eyes. He is not tall or imposing, but small and cat-like. He wears a blue and white checked shirt, a cream-colored Stetson, and well worn brown *chapajaros*. His clothes are dusty and threadbare from years of being a fugitive—bound to happen when you wear the same thing for years. Sonny's two Colt .45s, with smooth pearl handles, hang low on his thighs. What looks like a dimple in his cheek is, in reality, a bullet scar. And, like all cowboy heroes, he has a horse that is his best friend, his *compadre*, and his savior in many cases. Paint is a swift, agile, hardy, and incredibly intelligent pinto. He is a mustang and "desert-bred" and can outrun the wretched crook's horse, dodge bullets, and leap over brush all at the same time. Paint is always ready and available for Sonny; he never wanders off looking for food while Sonny is preoccupied with ugly, snarling gunmen. Instead, he waits quietly and patiently, in brush nearby, ready to leap out at Sonny's whistle. Paint jumps onto moving boxcars, comes back from the dead several times, gallops over hundreds of miles through moonless nights and cold snowy mountains, never stumbling and never tiring. Sonny loves Paint. He talks to his horse (many pulp heroes were quite chatty with their steeds) and Paint always nickers a knowledgeable answer. Sonny comes unglued when the safety of his horse is at stake. Awaiting what appears to be almost certain execution in one story, Sonny looks down from his jail cell at Paint, tied up at a railing outside, and cries because no provisions have been made for the care of his horse after he's gone.

Paul was the first to admit that Sonny was developed along the Billy the Kid format, a character that continued to live on in legend long after his death in 1881. He also confessed that "while writing about Sonny, I *was* Sonny. I was just immature enough mentally to be able to do it thoroughly and completely." Sonny's popularity, he guessed, was because "his adventures weren't simply a series of escapes from the manhunters who were after him. I tried to make it evident that he had been outlawed 'through no fault of his own.' He was especially popular when he helped others, which proved, if readers do identify themselves with the leading character, that the readers of *Wild West Weekly* were fundamentally a pretty good sort."

Another hero was riding on the horizon. The Fightin' Poet, who appeared in the July 20, 1929 issue, is an eccentric enigma who shows up at the Oriental Saloon wearing bright purple angora chaps, patent leather boots, and brand new cowboy hat, shirt, and vest. He keeps his mouth shut, even when goaded by curious cowboys who want to know who this bizarre stranger is that rode into their town. When he finally opens his mouth, it is only in the form of four-line verses, but ever mindful that his audience would be young boys reading his story in Prohibition times:

> Whiskey makes me very ill,
> Beer gives me quite a pain;
> So kindly fill a water glass,
> And I will be refreshed again!

The Fightin' Poet mutated into Johnny Socrates, otherwise known as Johnny Forty-Five, who answered in verse and was continually thrown into hot water by his bumbling sidekick, U.S. Deputy George Marshall Krumm. The magazine chose to published the Johnny Forty-Five stories under the house name Andrew Griffin.

Paul met his second wife, Mary, in Tucson, and they would shortly marry. Only a few months later, they moved to Long Beach, the first of many moves on the spur of the moment. In 1930, the country was just beginning to feel the effects of the 1929 stock market crash. But for Paul and Mary, life continued on as before. Renting a small bungalow on Sixth Street not too far from the beach, Paul churned out stories of Kid Wolf and Sonny Tabor, along with independent short stories, through 1930. Their financial good luck continued unabated. Photographs from that time show Paul in jodhpurs and Mary in fur, next to large convertibles, or riding horses in the desert, as if nothing had happened on Wall Street.

Oliphant doesn't mention the crash in a November 18, 1929 letter; as always, he was only concerned with Paul's production, and asked that Paul submit one short novel every week, rotating his steady characters, and also submit a short non-series story every other week. All in all, Oliphant was very pleased with his work; he mentions one time that a Sonny Tabor novelette he bought was a "corking good one." Amidst this merciless pace, Paul and Mary packed up their belongings and headed for Flagstaff, Arizona in the late fall of 1930. Paul wanted to experience the snow again, but they didn't even stay long enough to see the spring thaw. By March, 1931, they had traded in the cool climate and pine trees of Flagstaff for the blinding heat of Nogales at the opposite end of the state.

By the beginning of 1931, as America slid deeper into the Depression, Paul was making more money than ever. While bread lines grew longer throughout the country and banks failed on a daily basis, Paul averaged about $200 a story, and was bringing home between $400 and $500 a month, at least four times what the average worker in America was making, if they were working at all. Expensive homes, large cars, plenty of food, clothes, and liquor became the norm. Paul treated himself regularly by buying rare books for his growing collection. "I didn't suffer during the Depression, I'm ashamed to say," he wrote. It appeared that the paychecks from Street & Smith would never stop arriving.

Things seemed to calm down for a few months. He had a full house now. Besides John, called Jack, the family included Tom, who was born in 1930, and a daughter Pat, born in 1931. Paul's relationship with Street & Smith was solid. He had received a raise to a 1½¢ a word, which may not seem like much, but considering the volumes of words each story added up to, it meant another $50-$60 extra per story. The stories were showing up with reassuring regularity in *Wild West Weekly*, and Street & Smith's book publishing company elected to take five Sonny Tabor stories and publish them in book form. *Wanted—Sonny Tabor* (Chelsea House, 1931) was a compilation of "The Eleventh Notch", "Sonny Tabor, Deputy", "Sonny Tabor's Pine Coffin", "Sonny Tabor's Gun School", and "Sonny Tabor's Rodeo Stake".

In 1932 Paul and Mary moved to Bisbee, Arizona, a small mining town rich in history near the Mexican border. The town, insulated from the rest of the world by high rust-colored hills covered with yucca cactus and sagebrush, had remained virtually unchanged since its heyday in the 1880s. In the late 19th Century, mining had flourished there, and so had hangings, gunfights, drunkenness, and prostitution. Houses teetered on both sides of a narrow cañon, crammed into every single square inch on rocky, inhospitable hillsides. Comprised of a mixture of old shacks with paint peeling and little architectural dignity and well-preserved homes complemented by meticulous gardens, Bisbee had its own kind of flair.

But when Paul and Mary put up camp in 1932, Bisbee was suffering mightily because of the Depression. Even though it was one of the richest copper districts in the country, it was still a company town, run by the Phelps Dodge Company that owned the largest hotel in town, the hospital, department store, and the library. After the stock market crashed, production plummeted in almost all facets of American manufacturing, including the mining business. The local economy foundered, businesses faltered, and workers languished, waiting for work that never came. Eventually townspeople abandoned their hillside homes and moved away, never to return.

As it was, by 1932, almost no one in the country was immune from the Depression. Now, even the pulp magazine industry was feeling the effects. Oliphant departed from his usually polite and detached business tone to write a personal letter to Paul, the sole purpose being to lament about the conditions in New York:

> Are there any signs of a depression down there? Or do you only read about it in the papers? . . . The 2¢ *hombres* are taking a terrible shellacking these days. Every few days, there is a big *boom!* and another magazine has exploded. One publisher killed five in a day. Another has killed off all his pulps.

But Paul's life in Bisbee seemed to be a million miles from the country's woes. Paul and Mary were enamored with the town and the surrounding valley, flanked by mountain ranges on the western and eastern sides. Better yet, Tombstone, home of the gunfight at the OK Corral and a monument to the myth of the American West, was only a few miles away. By 1930, Tombstone had lost some of its luster, but Main Street was still dressed with wooden sidewalks and historical buildings and was still a tourist destination. For Paul, pulp stories lurked in the alleys, just waiting to be written. Living in Bisbee and using Tombstone as a creative source would end up as being one of the wisest moves Paul ever made as a writer. The rich history and heart-stopping landscape would reverberate in his writing for years.

Paul continued to crank out the stories, but he had been writing for Street & Smith for four years at this point, and he was getting tired. For one thing, for almost three solid years, Paul had written only Kid Wolf, Sonny Tabor, and an occasional Johnny Forty-Five story. Ninety-one stories would get published without any variation in the characters.

"[There] is a danger of a man going stale," Oliphant warned, "if he keeps plugging away at the same three characters year in and year out, as you have been doing." He suggested that Paul write for one of the weaker members of the Street & Smith stable, a magazine called *Top-Notch*. Paul didn't take him up on the offer; chances are he had enough work to do and writing for another pulp wasn't exactly what he had in mind to alleviate his mental exhaustion. To help things, Paul found a separate cabin in Madera Cañon, where the weather was a little more forgiving and where he could escape the searing heat and write. But eventually Bisbee's newness wore off. At the end of 1933, Paul and the family packed up the Cadillac and moved to Portal, Arizona.

"I remember sometimes we moved in the middle of the night," his daughter Pat recalled. Her father never revealed his reasons for uprooting them so often and so abruptly. Concluding that they were leaving to skip out on rent would seem to run contrary to their moderately affluent lifestyle, where Paul was making more money than many town mayors, bankers, and doctors. Houses were always rented, because Paul didn't want to be tied down to a piece of real estate. Moreover, they were always rented furnished, so that their transitions could be as effortless as possible. Even their own personal possessions, such as dishes, lamps, or pictures, would be left behind. If Mary protested, Paul declared: "Don't worry about it! We can always buy more. I'll always make enough money." The only thing that Paul insisted on taking was, of course, his rare book collection. But the truth was Paul never managed his money properly and usually spent like a sailor on leave, a habit that would catch up with him later in life. But he also felt that it wasn't his obligation as an artist to be fiscally responsible.

The next few years were spent moving across southern California, as Paul continued to "write for the hungry maw of *Wild West Weekly*." He branched out and wrote more independent short stories in 1934 and 1935. He contributed to *Wild West Weekly*'s signature feature of partnering two or more heroes, that usually were featured in their own short novels, into collaborative stories. Some of these collaborations featured Sonny Tabor with other *Wild West Weekly* heroes like Pete Rice, Billy West, and the Circle J folks. Most of the time the magazine credited both writers in the byline, such as Cleve Endicott and Ward Stevens, but often these collaborations were really written entirely by Paul. It was inevitable that Kid Wolf and Sonny would match up, and they did in the September 7, 1935 issue with "Kid Wolf Rounds Up Sonny Tabor", included in this book. It was one of the most memorable of the collaborations, according to Red Boggs in *The Pulp Western*.

In 1936, the family left San Diego, alighted briefly in Ocean Beach for the summer, and then moved to Santa Fe, despite never having set foot in New Mexico. They rented a glorious pueblo home amidst the piñon trees at 7,000 feet altitude that had a fireplace in each room and was furnished with handmade furniture. Paul plunked his typewriter down in the magnificent library and frequented local bars when he didn't feel like working. He never felt comfortable in Santa Fe, however, because of the established artistic community there that looked down on industrial hacks. Suddenly he was made aware of the chasm between his profession and that of those who wrote for more serious endeavors, such as the "slick" magazines: "I was living in a community where a sharp distinction was made, socially, between pulp writers and—well, writers who amounted to something, writers who "counted."

After a few months, Paul couldn't take much more of Santa Fe. They were in New Mexico less than a year before moving back to Long Beach. By then, Paul was juggling five characters—Sonny Tabor, Kid Wolf, Freckles Malone, Johnny Forty-Five, and King Kolt—and also writing short stories, many under his own name. For several years he had worked at a pace of one novelette or an independent story every week. He was suffering from bouts of what was called neuralgia then, a painful nerve disorder. Paul would continue to have trouble with neuralgia for at least the rest of his pulp career. At one point, he dictated his stories, and Oliphant urged him to consider bringing in other writers to help out with Sonny Tabor and Kid Wolf stories, but he would never stop being the original creator.

By June 1937, when they reached Laguna Beach, California, Paul had changed residences fifteen times since his career had started with Street & Smith in 1928. The ghost towns of Blackhawk and Central City must have seemed light years away. During the Depression, Laguna Beach was hardly a place indicative of the rest of the country. Rather, it was a magnet for writers, artists, movie stars, and those who drifted into town to check out the scene. Filmmakers from Hollywood continually set up camp around the shimmering bay. Paul was relieved, however, to see that the town didn't seem to have the atmosphere of elitism that Santa Fe had. He gravitated to the offbeat casual lifestyle. Laguna was perfect for him; there were plenty of corner bars where he could plant himself and pontificate to anyone who would listen. He could usually find a few barflies that gave him audience, especially when he was buying the drinks. Many friends showed up while the family was in Laguna, and the atmosphere soon took on the air of a permanent holiday.

But the good times quickly wore off as Paul's drinking worsened. Laguna Beach may have been known as a relaxing vacation haven for most people, but it was a disaster for the Powers family. Twelve-year-old Jack would disappear for days at a time to escape his father's binges and the subsequent explosive home life. Paul admitted that he had to get out of Laguna because the atmosphere was "not conducive to hard work." For one thing, "friends were always dropping in with a bottle, or still worse, without one."

Paul was concerned when George Campbell Smith, last in a long line of Smiths heading the Street & Smith dynasty, passed away in 1937. Paul sensed that the inevitable transition in power would drastically alter the company's philosophy of doing business and its interactions with its authors. Yet, at that point, Paul didn't put too much energy into worrying about it. There wasn't enough time, for one thing. 1938 was one of the best years for Sonny Tabor stories, one of which is included in this volume, "Sonny Tabor and the Border Blackbirds". There were many more, including "Sonny Tabor Rides with Death", "Sonny Tabor Tracks a Wolf Pack", and "Sonny Tabor's Sheriff Pard", this last one a collaboration featuring Sonny Tabor and Pete Rice, another hero of *Wild West Weekly* who was so popular among readers that Street & Smith had launched *Pete Rice Magazine* in 1933. It had a run of thirty-two issues before it was absorbed, along with Pete Rice as a character, back into *Wild West Weekly*.

But by 1938, no one could ignore the signs that the pulp industry was changing. The country was slowly recovering from the Depression, and people were returning to work. Wage earners even had a few dollars left over for entertainment, so people could go to movies now, go out to eat, buy a radio for the living room, and buy "slick" magazines now and then. Changes in the nation's taste, the improving economy, and the comic book's ascent in popularity (an event that *Wild West Weekly* took very seriously, and they eventually added a comic strip to the magazine's regular features) all hurt the industry.

Pulp publishers scrambled to find ways to keep their audience. *Wild West Weekly* encouraged Paul to alter Sonny's lifestyle drastically. As a result, Sonny Tabor was pushed into a litany of permutations that would have exhausted and confused any superhero. First, in March 1939, he is pardoned by his long-time friend, Governor John Hatfield, in "Sonny Tabor Wins a Pardon", and then in May he is kicked upstairs to join the Arizona Rangers in "Sonny Tabor Joins the Rangers". Eventually he leaves the Rangers, and goes back to his old bandit ways, but in reality he is an undercover agent, a premise that lasted for several years. During all of this frantic activity, he also manages to snag a steady girlfriend, Rita. This last accomplishment didn't go over well with readers. Paul had to do some major work to get his character back in readers' good graces: "I couldn't marry the fellow off, and neither could I permit him to consummate his love in an unethical way—not in *Wild West*! I suffered as much as Sonny Tabor, I think, during those months."

Paul welcomed some of the changes. Sonny and Kid Wolf were allowed to take on a more worldly air, and were even allowed to take a drink occasionally. Card playing was now an accepted pastime, rather than something that Sonny always frowned upon because of its gambling dangers. Heroes were even allowed to curse once in a while, instead of the "Blast you!" that had been the euphemistic alternative, and even the word "blood" was now permitted.

Then, in 1939, Ronald Oliphant left Street & Smith.

The departure of Oliphant was a huge blow to all of the writers at *Wild West Weekly*. His replacement, Francis Stebbins, stayed a few years, until the third and final editor, John Burr, took over in 1941. Burr, an experienced editor who had revitalized Street & Smith's *Western Story Magazine*, was now to bring to the Western fiction in *Wild West Weekly* a more mature, adult-oriented realism. Effective he may have been; diplomatic he wasn't. No longer did Paul have the luxury of dealing with an editor who would always, even in tense moments, maintain his gentlemanly composure. All of a sudden, getting his stories into the magazine wasn't guaranteed. Paul received his first rejection from the magazine in over twelve years. "[It] seemed that my story had no plot, and my style was wrong and full of clichés." He grudgingly conceded that Burr was somewhat justified in his criticism, but his simple, conversational style was what his readers liked. "My readers had told me that I was easy to read, and I wanted to stay that way. They don't want to think; they want to be entertained. They know what they want and they insist on getting it." Even though Burr complained about the juvenility of Paul's stories, he continued to buy them, and all of Paul's characters stayed with the magazine.

Pulp magazines continued to decline in popularity after Pearl Harbor and the war effort made it increasingly difficult for many publishers to continue. Boys that had read the magazines on their porches during the Depression were now off to war, and keeping up with their pulp heroes' adventures was probably not one of their top priorities. The war effort dominated all forms of popular culture; over the years, war magazines had encroached on the newsstands, and by the beginning years of World War II, combat stories had become popular. Rationing began of many materials such as steel, aluminum, nylon, rubber, and paper. Shortages affected the entire newspaper and magazine industry. For many of the pulps, the paper shortage was the final blow. Between the paper shortage and the diminishing audience, many pulp magazines quietly signed off, or cut back on the frequency and size of issues. *Wild West Weekly* was no exception. Gradually, over the next few years, the magazine cut back on its size and even changed its name to *Wild West* when it was no longer published weekly. Paul was told to shorten the story lengths. The illustrations and superb covers that had always marked the magazine were beginning to be replaced by reprints from the 1930s. The interior illustrations were taken from the *Western Story* and *Cowboy Stories* illustration banks. Eventually *Wild West* shifted from being a biweekly to a monthly.

By this time, the family was in Orange, California, living comfortably in a stately Craftsman-style home with an imposing portico and a backyard full of fruit and avocado trees. Jack, Tom, and Pat enjoyed their time there—for once, it seemed, as if they were going to stay in one place for a while. Jack graduated from high school in 1942 and promptly joined the Navy under age, just like his father had. Jack, however, saw real combat as a medic, and eventually was awarded a Bronze Star for heroic duty during the battle of Tarawa in the Pacific. He had plans to become a doctor, and that made Paul very happy; even though he hadn't fulfilled his father's wish in becoming a doctor, both of his sons were well on their way to that goal. Still, financial troubles were mounting. Paul continually had to ask for advances and eventually they moved into a small and much less luxurious house on the poorer side of Orange.

The last Sonny Tabor story, "The Devil Rides a Pinto", appeared in the August 14, 1943 issue. Then, in November,

1943 the magazine published its last issue. The cover was simply illustrated with a cowboy on a pinto, forging a creek, looking back toward his pursuer. Paul had two stories in the issue. The cover copy proclaimed that there was a "flaming" Johnny Forty-Five story called "Hog Legs for Range Hogs" inside, and another story, "Death Blots the Brands", was credited to Paul under his real name. Close to the end of "Death Blots the Brands" a small sidebar was inserted that read:

> Because of the drastic necessity for the conservation of paper and because we are doing everything in our power to co-operate with our government in winning this war, we announce, with regrets, that with this issue *Wild West* will suspend publication for the duration.

While the rest of the country had seen the worst of financial hardship during the Great Depression, Paul's own financial depression was just beginning. The next ten years would be some of the family's hardest. Still, he hunkered down and began work on what he had dreamed of doing for so long, writing a novel based on his father's life as a pioneer doctor. This would be a different Western, and would feature Paul's extensive knowledge of Western history and frontier medicine. It would be unique, and would surely pull his family out of its financial doldrums.

Meanwhile, to keep the family in shoes, Paul sporadically sold stories to those pulps that had managed to stay in business, such as *Western Story*, now a monthly, and *Ranch Romances*. Judging from the meager amount of correspondence from *Western Story* in Paul's papers, the volume he produced for them was a fraction of what he had written for

Wild West Weekly. Each pulp commanded its own style from its writers, and Paul needed to adjust his style of the last fifteen years in order to fit in with the demands of these more famous and prestigious pulps. So Paul, now in his forties, had to start all over again as an apprentice writer. He struggled to write stories that might or might not get published, and wondered how he would pay the rent.

When *Doc Dillahay* was finally published by Macmillan in 1949, despite receiving good reviews across the country and being reprinted as a paperback under the title *Six Gun Doctor*, it did not become the bestseller Paul had hoped for. Nevertheless, Paul always prided himself on the fact that he was able to write an atypical Western that featured frontier medicine and didn't have the usual "gunslinger" or "cowboy and Indians" plot. Macmillan certainly believed in the book, and, despite its meager sales, the publisher was encouraged and asked Paul to start on a sequel. He did, and submitted the first two chapters to the editor after a few months. But the book was rejected because, the Macmillan editor felt, the story didn't sufficiently fall into their guidelines for Western fiction.

Eventually Paul and Mary, their kids grown, moved to the Bay area to be closer to their sons. Jack was in medical school in San Francisco by this time, and Tom was pre-med at Berkeley. Pat married and stayed in southern California. Perhaps the Bay area would promise to be another fresh place where Paul could start writing again. But he sold very little, and what little money they lived on was from Paul's book trades and Mary's sporadic work in factories or as a housekeeper. All of the money from the pulps was long gone. Times were very lean for quite a few years: "What couldn't I do with the $800 month I could always make, if pressed, in the old pulps. But I had to pay for those 'easy' years; how much longer must I pay?" he wrote in 1951. Eventually he found work at a bookstore on Telegraph Avenue close to the UC Berkeley campus and became known for his knowledge of Western Americana.

Another book collector, Robert Hawley, recalled Paul as having a dignified air, despite the fact that he wore the same cardigan sweater. He kept to himself, even when the two shared a seat on bus rides, but he would perk up when discussing rare books or his love of history of the West. And as reserved as he was, Hawley fondly remembered occasionally sharing a whiskey bottle that Paul had stashed behind the store counter. Paul never told Hawley that he had been a pulp writer. In fact, he had refused to let his children read pulp magazines, and he never kept a single issue featuring his own work. Yet he kept all of his papers from those years, including 180 letters he had received from Ronald Oliphant and other editors from 1928 through 1943, an unpublished memoir entitled *Pulp Writer,* and several unpublished manuscripts. He never published another book after *Doc Dillahay.* He did attempt to write another called *The Strange Case of Christopher Sperm.* God only knows the theme; Paul burned the manuscript after Macmillan rejected it.

In 1964, the family suffered a major blow when Jack, who was my father, died at the age of thirty-nine. His promising career as a physician had fizzled after medical school primarily because he had picked up a drinking habit that would, in very short time, engulf his life. The last six years of Jack's life were spent trying to kick his drinking habit but he only became more entwined in a downward spiral of failed marriages and state institutions. Tom and Pat, however, went on to have successful careers—Tom as a psychiatrist and Pat as a university administrator—and happy family lives. But it was clear to Paul's family that he never recovered from his elder son's death. He drank constantly, alienating himself from the rest of the family.

Paul died in 1971, his death somewhat a mystery. The cause of death was listed on the death certificate as a "head injury from an unknown collapse or fall," and Mary, devastated, never wanted to discuss it. Where or how he fell would never be known. Ironically, his death certificate noted that alcohol, his nemesis throughout his life, was not present in his blood at the time of death. Afterwards, his *Wild West Weekly* papers were piled into two boxes and left in his daughter's attic for almost thirty years.

One day at Smith, around the time that I received that first package from Syracuse containing the eighty receipts, I started another search on the Internet. I wanted to find out more about my grandfather's hometown of Little River. After a few minutes, I found a Kansas genealogy Web site, where you could post notices asking for information on relatives. What the heck, I thought, it's free. I typed in a short notice saying that I was looking for any information about a Paul Powers, son of the Little River town doctor at the turn of the century, or Paul's son Jack. I doubted that I would get any response. I was asking for information on people that lived a century ago, after all. I left for class, promptly forgetting about it. But the next day, when I returned, there was an e-mail from a distant cousin. He knew of another cousin that had extensively researched the Powers family. Within another day, I had the addresses for my Aunt Pat and Uncle Tom, who I hadn't seen in thirty-five years, and the addresses of my grandfather's brother George and his sister Phyllis, both still alive and well.

That summer, I sat in my aunt's dining room and together we opened those two boxes that had been stuffed away in her attic for so many years. The very first piece of paper I picked up was a small gray memo, dated January 16, 1934, from *Wild West Weekly*, addressed to Paul Powers, Portal, Arizona. It began:

We were pleased to purchase the Sonny Tabor novelette. . . .

The Eleventh Notch

Paul S. Powers probably didn't have any idea that the hero in "The Eleventh Notch", his thirty-seventh story published in *Wild West Weekly*, would end up being the first of 130 Sonny Tabor stories. He was twenty-four and still had plenty of youth, exuberance, and optimism—traits reflected in Sonny's character and probably what made the outlaw hugely popular with readers.

Fans and scholars have speculated over the years as to how Powers came up with the name Sonny Tabor. The real story has nothing to do with symbolism or Western history. Powers recalled: "The 'talkie' of *Sonny Boy* [Warner, 1929] was being shown in Tucson that week, and it's likely the suggestion for the first name came from that, and Tabor from the Colorado Tabors." He had frequented the Tabor Theatre while living in Denver in the early 1920s, and the name stuck.

"The Eleventh Notch" was published under the magazine's house name, Ward M. Stevens, that Powers had used four times before and that was also used by other writers as well. But when both Sonny Tabor and Kid Wolf picked up speed, the Ward M. Stevens pseudonym was assigned exclusively to Paul S. Powers. He would use it for the Sonny Tabor, Kid Wolf, and Freckles Malone stories for the magazine's duration.

I

An hour before noon, six men were climbing a hill known as the Hacha, fifteen miles north of the Sonora border. They had tied their horses to the mesquites in the arroyo below and were mounting on foot, as the going was extremely difficult. The little hill was not high, but its name, translated from the Spanish, described it. It meant "Hatchet", and the rocks that formed it were cruel and sharp.

The man leading the way was Ed Stewart, the owner of the Triangle Cross, a ranch many miles to the northward. He was past sixty, but no one would have guessed it from his wiry build and easy, graceful strength. The hair showing under his big Stetson was nearly white, but age had left few other marks on his face.

"Hurry on, boys!" he called back over his shoulder. "We're nearly up, and I'm anxious to see what that mound is."

The foreman of the outfit was next behind him. He was a loose-limbed cowpuncher of forty with thin, tightly set lips and narrow eyes.

"I told you what I thought it looked like from below, Stewart," he grunted.

"A grave?" muttered his employer thoughtfully. "I wonder. What poor *hombre* could be buried up here?"

One of the Triangle Cross riders—a clean-cut young fellow of twenty—spoke up: "The only thing I know is that it wasn't there five months ago when I rode up from Nogales with those horses of Bradford's."

"We'll soon be there," returned Stewart, a worried look creeping into his eyes. "But if it's really a grave, I guess there won't be no way o' tellin' what. . . ." He broke off, but the other men knew what was on his mind.

A few steps more, and they had reached the summit of the little desert hill and were looking at what they had seen from below. The mound of rocks was perhaps seven feet long and three wide, and it was indeed a grave, for at the bend of it was a forked stick as a sort of marker. Whoever was resting there, however, had not been buried. Instead, the stones had been piled upon his body. To prove this, signs around the grave showed that pack rats had been at it. Scattered here and there were shreds of clothing.

The men who had climbed to see it, and especially the old ranchman, were visibly affected by the gruesome sight. Moffitt, the youngest cowboy, shivered and turned away.

"Look," said Ross, the Triangle Cross foreman. "What's that hangin' to that head marker by a string?"

"Why, it's an empty shell!" exclaimed one of the cowpunchers. His face was a little white, as if he were expecting something.

Stewart reached over and pulled the empty cartridge from the half-rotted bit of string. He turned the bit of brass over in his palm and shook it. A tiny folded slip of white paper slid out.

Stewart spread it out with trembling fingers. It was an ordinary cigarette paper, but something was written on it in pencil. The old man held it closer to his eyes. Then he stepped back with a short sharp cry. His faded blue eyes had suddenly clouded over with grief and horror.

"It's Bob!" he gasped. "Bob's buried here! Read it!"

He passed the paper over to the others. The short and grim message, in small, cramped handwriting, read as follows:

ROB'T STEWART, DIED APRIL 11
SONNY TABOR
NO. 11

"The date is right," said Stewart in a bitter voice. "Bob disappeared on April Eleventh."

"But . . . but what does this all mean?" Moffitt demanded, puzzled. "What does Sonny Tabor mean? And number eleven?"

The foreman turned to Stewart. "You know, don't you, Stewart?" he asked.

The old man nodded, his face darkening with rage. "Yes," he snapped out, "I think I do."

"Sonny Tabor, the outlaw?" one of the cowboys ejaculated.

"Nobody else," the foreman snarled. "It's his work, all right. And this explains where the payroll went three months ago."

Every one of the six, with the exception of young Moffitt, had heard much of Sonny Tabor—one of the most-feared desperadoes of the Southwest. The very name was enough to chill the hearts of those who had heard of his deeds. The name, Sonny, sounded mild enough, but no one along the border was so fast and sure with a six-shooter, or so fearless in fight. He was the thorn in the sides of all law officers from Yuma to El Paso.

"But I still don't savvy what he means by number eleven," somebody said.

Ross proceeded to explain in detail. "It's as plain as the nose on your face. Every one along the border knows that Sonny Tabor's killed ten men. Well, Bob here made number eleven. It's his eleventh man."

Young Moffitt looked horrified. "And he boasts of his killin's like that?" he cried. "Why . . . why, the cut-throat. Eleven men. He deserves a rope if ever a man did. Sonny Tabor. I'd like to have my hands on him."

Old Stewart's face was like a thundercloud. "Someday I

mean to have my hands on him. And when I do. . . ."

Three months before, Stewart's son Bob had disappeared. He had been carrying the payroll money from Desert City to the Triangle Cross, and he had ridden alone. He had left town on time, but he had never reached the ranch. The payroll, all in gold, had disappeared along with the messenger who was to deliver it. For weeks, Stewart and his riders had scoured the hills and deserts, searching for some trace or clue, but to no avail. It was as if the earth had swallowed horse and rider. And now, unexpectedly, Stewart had found his son.

"I'm sorry . . . for his mother's sake," he said brokenly. "It will . . . nearly kill her. But at that, I guess it will be a relief, after all this heart-breakin' uncertainty. One thing's botherin' me now."

"What is it?" Ross wanted to know.

"I want to be *sure* that it's Bob under there. I want to know for certain. I'm afraid to look myself. I haven't the courage. But you boys all knew him as well as me. I want you to look under there and find out. I'll be down below with the hosses."

"Sure, Mister Stewart," Moffitt said gently. "We understand."

The old rancher was waiting down in the mesquite when they returned to him. All were carrying their Stetsons, baring their heads to the hot sun in respect for the dead.

"It's him, all right," the foreman said. "We all looked. There ain't no mistake."

The others nodded.

Stewart placed the empty cartridge that had been on the grave into his vest pocket. Then he slowly mounted his horse, and the others followed his example. All were silent.

Moffitt's eyes were moist with tears. Bob Stewart had been his especial friend.

The old ranchman shook his fist in the air. "Sonny Tabor," he snarled. "Someday we'll meet and, when we do, Colts will blaze. I hope I live to see Bob's killer brought to justice." Then he sighed, the light faded from his eyes, and he turned to his men. "Back to the Triangle Cross, boys," he ordered in a firm voice.

II

Ma Stewart was busy cleaning up the Triangle Cross ranch house. She had worked all afternoon tidying up the long, low-ceilinged rooms, for she expected her husband back from his journey south at any hour. Mrs. Ed Stewart was a kind-faced, motherly woman who looked younger than her fifty-odd years. Her rounded arms were still plump, and she was as full of good humor and bustling energy as ever.

Everyone loved Ma Stewart. They couldn't help it. She was famed the country around for her cooking, her smiles, and her cheery ways. That was why they called her "Ma". She was the ranch mother—a product of the West fully as much as her husband Ed.

With the last few months, sorrow and tragedy had come to Mrs. Stewart. Bob was her only son, and he was gone. One by one, hopes had faded and left grief in their place. Weeks ago, Ma Stewart had realized that she was never to see her boy again.

It was a hard country, full of many dangers. Many things could have happened to Bob; he might have been shot down by renegade Apaches, or robbed and killed by bandits. But one thing Ma knew—her boy was dead. She realized it in her heart, for, alive, he would have returned to her. But she had borne up bravely under her terrible loss. For her husband's sake, her smile was the same as ever. And time, however slowly, heals all wounds.

As she worked, she often went to the little window that looked on the trail leading to Chollaville. Her husband and the cowboys were overdue. Already appetizing smells drifted from the kitchen.

The Triangle Cross *hacienda* was at the foot of a mountain pass. On the westward, high cave-like cliffs towered into the sunset, studded here and there with armless giant cacti. Between the two walls, a faint trail led above and over the range. The Chollaville road led in another direction.

On her last trip to the window, Ma Stewart beamed happily. "Well, I declare," she said to herself. "There they come at last."

A cloud of dust had appeared far down the Chollaville road, and before many minutes the outlines of fast-riding horsemen appeared in it. Ma counted them as they gradually drew nearer.

"Six . . . seven . . . eight . . . nine." She wondered: "Why, who could be with them?"

Besides her husband and Ross—his foreman—there were only four Triangle Cross men, she well knew. Puzzled, she watched closely.

Why, it wasn't the Triangle Cross outfit, at all. The men were all strangers. Could anything have happened to her husband? Much worried, she went outside, walked down to the road, and waited.

The horsemen had been riding hard, for their mounts were foam-covered. Seeing Mrs. Stewart standing in front of the *hacienda,* they whirled to a stop and dismounted.

The woman saw now that the foremost rider was Jim

Nowell, the sheriff. She had met him several times before. He came toward her, doffing his big hat gallantly.

"How are you, Ma?" he asked genially.

She answered his greeting and asked breathlessly: "Who are all these men, Mister Nowell? What has happened? Did you meet Ed and the boys on the way?"

"These men are a posse," explained the big peace officer, "and we think we have an outlaw cornered at the pass. We didn't see anything of your husband, ma'am."

The ranch wife was greatly relieved and invited them all into the house for supper.

"That's just it, Missus Stewart," said the sheriff earnestly. "We have every reason to believe that the man we are after is headed down this way from the mountain pass. We want to hide in your house and wait until he rides past, then we'll get him."

Ma looked him straight in the eyes. "Who is this outlaw you're after?"

"A man known as Sonny Tabor," Nowell replied.

"And he's alone?"

"He's a lone wolf, yes," Nowell told her.

Ma's eyes could flash, and they flashed now. "There's nine of you!" she cried. "Nine against one. And you mean to shoot him down in ambush. No, siree. You don't use my house to trap him, Mister Sheriff. I won't stand for it. You all ought to be ashamed of yourselves. You're cowards, every last one of you."

Nowell flinched, and his face flushed under this tirade. "But you don't understand, Ma," he explained. "This Sonny Tabor is a dangerous man . . . a killer. Why, he's accounted for ten men. And we represent the law. Of course, we won't shoot him down cold. We'll give him a chance to surrender, but if he won't, we'll have to shoot. Don't you see?"

Ma did *not* see, and she was not slow in telling the sheriff that she didn't. In spite of all arguments, Nowell was forced to retire. He called his men together for a conference, after Ma had returned to the house.

"She's on her high hoss for some reason," he said. "A mighty fine woman, but you know how women are. Too soft-hearted."

"We ought to force our way in thar, anyways," a member of the posse blurted out.

"No, we don't," the sheriff snapped out sharply. "But I guess we can hide ourselves around here somewhere without usin' the house. We've got a positive tip that Sonny is ridin' this way, and I don't mean to let him slip through my fingers this time. He's due through here any minute now, as I've figgered it out."

"Well, what'll we do?" questioned a deputy.

The sheriff considered. "There's nine of us," he said. "Kelly, Jacobs, and McRobb will hide over there behind that mesquite corral. Charley and me will get in that wagon . . . the box will keep us from bein' seen. Taylor, Watson, and Lopez will stand in the doorway of that little ruined adobe. Moore, suppose you lie down behind that cactus clump. Be careful, all of you, to keep under cover."

"Do we shoot on sight?" someone asked.

Nowell shook his head. "There's goin' to be no blunders!" he barked. "We'll get him dead if we can't get him alive. Odds or no odds, he'll shoot it out. But no one will fire until I say the word. I'll give him his chance to surrender. When you do fire, shoot to kill. Savvy?"

The posse signified that they fully understood their orders, and took their positions without delay.

III

While the death trap was being set in the valley below, a lone rider was climbing down the narrow trail in the mountain gap. In spite of the roughness of the dangerous path, he was splitting the wind. The horse he rode was a speedy, powerful pinto, desert-bred. Horse, rider, and silver-mounted saddle alike were covered with a layer of dust, for they had been traveling for hours.

Few knew Sonny Tabor's real age, which was twenty. Some thought him even younger, but most of those who knew his record would have placed him as at least five years beyond his teens. He had always been called Sonny, but nobody knew if this was his real name. It fitted him. His face was boyish, always smiling. He didn't look like an outlaw or a dangerous man. His frank blue eyes were innocent and mild, his mouth clean-cut and pleasing. One cheek was marked with a bullet scar, however, and there was a certain alertness about him that attracted attention. His dress, from his small high-heeled half boots to his creamy Stetson, was neat. He wore a dark vest over a blue-and-white-checked shirt, unbuttoned. About his slim hips, a cartridge belt was buckled, and from it swung two big, solid-framed .45s. On the pinto, in a leather scabbard, was a Winchester rifle.

Sonny Tabor had just had a narrow escape. On the other side of the range, he had been nearly cornered by three law officers. But by hard riding and superb horsemanship, he had given them the slip, and now, as far as he knew, he was on the way to the desert beyond and comparative safety.

The sun beat down fiercely, and the rocks reflected it into a blazing glare. Both rider and mount were in need of rest and water. Sonny knew that he would find the latter, at least, in the valley. From the trail he could see the plain and rolling mesa below, blotted out here and there with tricky mirages of false water. An occasional giant cactus rose before him, and he guided his horse around it without slackening his pace. The valley beneath became more fully outlined now, and he could see the Triangle Cross buildings with the plain of mesquite and creosote bush beyond, relieved here and there with erect wands of ocotillo.

Just before descending the pass, Sonny Tabor drew his horse to a halt. He examined the Triangle Cross *hacienda* attentively. Nobody about the place. Nobody at the corral or at the fenced water hole. Still Sonny Tabor waited, with eyes open. There was many a bullet with Sonny's name on it, and he was not a man to take chances. For fully ten minutes, he waited, searching the floor of the valley beneath.

Somehow, Sonny felt a premonition of danger. He couldn't have told exactly why, but he felt that all was not well. It was necessary, however, for him to go on. There was no turning back now. Dangerous or not, he had to keep going.

"What do you think about it, Chief?" he asked his horse in a low whisper.

The horse stamped its forehoof uneasily. Sonny considered thoughtfully for a moment, and then laughed.

"Well, we're goin' down there, anyway," he said. "It's just got to be done."

He examined his Colts, wiped the dust from them, and returned them to their holsters. Then he lay the reins on the left side of his horse's neck and touched him with the spur.

Slowly they climbed down the pass, cutting this way and that, but going always down. Beneath them, the big adobe *hacienda* lay baking in the sun. Two ravens settled in the stunted white cottonwood near the water hole. All seemed well.

Twenty minutes brought them out of the pass, and here the trail widened and led directly past the Triangle Cross *hacienda*. Sonny increased his pace until he was almost within a stone's throw of the ranch house.

Suddenly a voice rang out, loud and sharp: "Sonny Tabor, you're under arrest! Throw up your hands!"

The voice came from an old wagon near the mesquite wood corral, and Sonny, instead of obeying the order, whirled his horse about and drew one of his .45s at the same instant. His revolver flashed fire and smoke. At almost the same instant, two jets of flame leaped from the wagon box. Splinters flew from the sideboards of the wagon. Somebody in it was hit, for a cry rang out.

At the same instant, the guns of the three men hidden behind the corral fence began to sputter lead. Sonny, shooting quickly and from the hip, threw two shots at the puffs of smoke, and put the rowels to his horse. But it was nine to one! Taylor, Watson, and Lopez, until now hidden inside the walls of the roofless abode, opened fire. Their guns smashed lead all about Sonny. From behind a cactus clump, Moore, armed with a long-barreled six-shooter, got into action. His gun joined the thundering chorus.

Sonny whirled in the saddle, and, snapping a deadly shot from the level of his thigh, silenced this new enemy with a bullet that ripped through the cactus into Moore's body. Sonny, seeing that he must fight it out, swung out his other .45 and turned it loose to crash quick thunder. Bits of mesquite wood flew from the corral fence. One of the men hidden there suddenly jumped up and ran, stumbling, half crazed from a bullet that had nipped him in the right side. Sonny Tabor made dust spurts leap from the adobe ruin, and the men there began to scramble for better cover.

But the fight could not last. Already, two bullets had gone through the high crown of the young outlaw's hat. Another had shot away his saddle pommel. A leaden slug ripped into his horse, striking the animal in the ribs. The pinto shivered and went down on his forelegs. Sonny scrambled out of the saddle just as the animal dropped. Another bullet tore its way through the horse's chest, killing him instantly.

Sonny threw himself behind the body of the animal for shelter. Unhorsed, there seemed no way of escape now.

"We've got him, boys!" Sheriff Nowell exulted.

IV

The man in the wagon with the sheriff was wounded, but Nowell kept up a heavy fire, sending bullet after bullet tearing into the dead horse. Sonny looked around for a better hiding place, but found none.

Keeping flat, he reloaded his Colts. For years his horse, Chief, had served him, and now, even after death, the animal was serving him. Slug after slug tore into the carcass. Spurts of sand were kicked up on all sides.

"Someone get around behind him!" Nowell yelled.

Sonny's guns were red-hot, but he fanned the hammers again relentlessly. No man of the posse dared to show himself for long. Sonny's aim was swift, deadly. Desperado or not, there was something heroic in the fight this boy was making against odds. He seemed to know no fear, although he was facing death every second.

Suddenly, in the gunfire, he heard a voice call out behind him—a woman's voice. In surprise, he turned his head a little. It was Ma Stewart. Braving the bullets that were flying about like mad hornets, and risking her life, she was at the window of the front room of the *hacienda*.

"Sonny!" she was crying. "Their horses! Their horses!"

She signaled to something on the far side of the house.

Sonny knew what she meant. The posse had left their mounts on the shady side of the long adobe building, so that they would be out of sight of anyone coming down through the pass. Dared he make a break for them? It meant almost certain death. But then, to remain where he was meant death, also. The dead horse was riddled with lead, and it was only a miracle that Sonny had not been hit thus far. But the minute he showed himself in the open, he knew that he would be a target for every gun.

He decided to risk making a dash for one of the posse horses. It was his only chance. In his heart he felt a tug of gratitude. To think that this woman, a stranger, would do this for him. Sonny had never known anything like this happen to him before. So few had been kind to him. Until now, it had seemed that the whole world was his enemy.

Taking a deep breath, he made a leap to his feet. As he did so, guns seemed to blaze from everywhere. As he ran, a bullet burned its way between his arm and body. Another fanned his ear. With a spurt of speed, he rounded the corner of the building.

The horses were there, and he threw himself desperately upon the nearest one. The animal reared back as he gave it the spur, but Sonny whirled around its head and urged the startled horse into a gallop.

The breath suddenly left Sonny's body as a terrific impact struck him in the right side of his back. It was followed by an agony that fairly numbed. Sonny realized that he had been hit and that the wound was bad. But he hung on and crouched even lower in the saddle.

Revolver shots still rang out behind him, but rapidly he was drawing away. Then there came a sudden lull in the shooting, and Sonny knew that the posse was mounting its horses to pursue him. Sonny had been fortunate in selecting the sheriff's own mount—the speediest of all of them. Even after hoof beats began to drum behind him, he drew off from the posse yard by yard.

Ed Stewart and his men were about a mile from the Triangle Cross, when they began to hear the sound of firing. Wondering what could be wrong at the ranch, they urged their mounts on at top speed, Ed Stewart in the lead.

The gunshots were louder as they neared the ranch, and suddenly Ross, the foreman, yelled: "Someone's comin' this way on a hoss, an' ridin' like mad!"

With an exclamation, the old rancher reined his mount and ordered his men to range themselves across the road.

"We'll see who it is!" he barked. "I'm plumb curious to know what's goin' on here."

The party strained their eyes ahead, trying to identify the figure that was riding so desperately toward them.

Suddenly Ross ripped out an oath. "It's Sonny Tabor!" With his words, he jerked out his gun.

Ed Stewart's lean features were convulsed with rage. He had gone white with fury at his foreman's words. Sonny Tabor, the outlaw—the murderer of his son!

"Here's where I even up Bob's bill," he jerked in a choked voice. "I was prayin' for this hour to come, and here it is. Let him have it."

The old man fired twice from the hip, then raised his Colt to the level of his eyes, took deliberate and careful aim, and emptied it straight at the oncoming rider. The others, too, had drawn and were now ripping bullets in Tabor's direction.

Sonny swerved his horse to one side. He hadn't expected this new menace. A bullet crashed through one leg, the terrific force of it nearly carrying him from his saddle. Another slug caught him—in the chest, this time. The impact knocked him from his horse, and he hung, head down, from one stirrup.

More dead than alive, he felt himself being dragged. Time after time his head struck the terrible cholla cactus that lined the road. The fearful spines seemed to be tearing his head from his body. All the while a sinister numbness was enveloping the upper part of his breast. Then the leather gave way, and he dropped. He rolled over a few times, tried to get on his feet, and fainted.

"We got him. We got the cowardly coyote," Ross snarled. "It was my bullet that knocked him off his hoss."

"Good work," Stewart said grimly.

They all dismounted and walked over to where Sonny Tabor lay. Face down, he was sprawled on the sand. The muscles of his lean back were twitching convulsively, and his clothing was soaked everywhere with red.

As contemptuously as if he were dealing with a dog, Stewart turned him over with his foot.

"He's alive," young Moffitt said in awed voice.

"Well, he's dyin'," growled Ross, "and it's a good thing, too, blast him." He ended his remarks with a string of oaths.

The posse, or what was left of the posse, rode up at this moment and dismounted. The sheriff explained to Stewart what had happened.

"He got Charley Foss and Ed Moore, Kelly's bad hurt. If you hadn't stopped him, I guess he'd've made his getaway. Reckon he's done for. I hoped he'd live to hang."

"He deserves all he got," Stewart said heavily, "and more." Then he proceeded to tell Sheriff Nowell of the finding of his son's body.

"Hmm," muttered the sheriff, "one more crime to chalk up on the kid's record. Well, I reckon he's paid, or will very shortly. So Sonny murdered your son. Queer. Your wife. . . ."

"Is she all right?" Stewart asked in an anxious voice.

"Shore," Nowell said in an embarrassed tone. "It ain't that. It's just that . . . well, she almost saved Sonny Tabor."

The sheriff told the astonished old ranchman what had happened.

"Ain't that just like a woman!" he ejaculated. "Ma's so tender-hearted. Don't want to see a fly get hurt. But when she knows that Sonny murdered Bob. . . ." He shook his head grimly.

Nowell and the members of the posse were examining Tabor's wounds. The lad was still unconscious and seemed likely to remain so until the end.

"Has he got a chance, do you think?" Moffitt asked.

In the eyes of the young cowpuncher was something very like admiration. In spite of the fact that this youthful desperado had shot one of his best friends—Bob Stewart—he could not help admiring the nerve this outlaw had displayed against such odds.

"He won't live the day out," was Nowell's opinion. "But, of course, the unexpected sometimes does happen. I ain't a doctor, but it 'pears to me he's shot up mighty bad. His chest is nearly blown away. Maybe we'd better carry him over to your place, Stewart."

Ross interrupted, his gaunt face livid with passion. "Don't you let 'em take that young whelp there, Stewart!

Why, he killed your boy. He's nothin' but a cut-throat and a killer."

But, in spite of the hate the old rancher had in his heart against the man who had shot his son, he was not without mercy. "Yes," he decided, "it's all right to take him back to the ranch. You can put him in the old blacksmith shop. I hope he gets well, so he can hang."

In a few minutes they were on their way back to the Triangle Cross, with Sonny Tabor hanging limply across the saddle. In spite of his reputation, there was one thing that could be said of the young outlaw. It was Sheriff Nowell himself who voiced it: "Anyways," he muttered thoughtfully, "the lad was one game kid."

V

Sonny Tabor was not put in the old blacksmith shop. Ma Stewart wouldn't listen to it, and as usual she had her way. Neither did she forgive her husband and the Triangle Cross men for shooting Sonny down after he had escaped from the posse. In fact, she wept over it, making old Ed feel very much like a dog that had been caught killing sheep.

"But he's as good as dead, Ma," he said. "You mustn't take him in the house."

"That's just it!" Ma stormed. "I want him in the house, so I can nurse him!"

"W-h-a-t?" the old ranchman almost shouted in his astonishment.

"I mean just what I said, Edward J. Stewart," she said calmly. "I hope to bring back the life you almost took from him. Do you think you did a very brave and noble thing when you shot this poor boy who was trying so hard to gain his freedom?"

It was on the tip of Ed Stewart's tongue to tell her that Sonny Tabor was the murderer of her own son. But he hadn't the courage just then. He knew how it would hurt her. Perhaps that piece of news had better wait until Sonny Tabor was dead and taken away. It would be easier for her.

So he allowed Ma to have own way, and gave the men directions to carry the wounded man into the best bedroom of the *hacienda*. There was no use arguing with Ma. Besides, she had called him Edward J. Stewart, and Ed recognized that as a danger signal.

Ma had already been busy with the other wounded man—Kelly, of the posse. He was not seriously hurt, and was stretched out on the portico. So now Ma turned her attention to Sonny Tabor. Somehow—perhaps because he reminded her so much of her lost son—her heart went out to him. White and colorless on the clean blankets of the big bed, he seemed so fragile that the pressure of a finger would have ended him. She cried out in horror at his terrible wounds, and at the bristle of cholla thorns that made his face look like a pincushion.

But Ma's sympathy went further than mere tears and laments. Without losing time, she flew about, heating water, making bandages and dressings. Like many a woman of the West, Ma Stewart was not afraid of wounds. She knew how to care for them, for she had seen many of them.

Ma's attentions caused a near fight. Ross was loud in his criticism of her actions and the young cowpuncher, Moffitt, resented his sneers deeply. The two were outside with the other men when Moffitt called the foreman down sharply: "I wish you'd keep your mouth shut for a while, Ross."

The foreman whirled on him viciously. "Oh, you do, do

you?" he leered. "For *dos reales* I'd knock your yeller head off."

"Suppose you try it," Moffitt invited.

Ross didn't try it. Instead, he began to bluster. "Well, I'll show you who I am around here. You're through. I'm handin' you your time tonight. You're fired!"

But the ranch owner himself had heard at least part of the conversation, and he interposed quickly. "Forget it, both of you," he ordered. "Ross, don't talk so much. I know that you cared a lot for my son, and you hate his murderer maybe just as much as me. But just keep quiet. Moffitt ain't fired as yet, if I know it."

So temporarily, at least, the trouble was settled, although not to Ross's satisfaction. He knew Stewart well enough, however, to turn on his heel and stalk away without further quibbling.

In the meantime, Ma was doing her best with Sonny Tabor. His condition was critical, and an ordinary man would have died almost immediately from the wounds he had received. But Sonny had a more-than-average physical stamina. Although at the point of death from shock and his wounds, he clung to life, somehow.

All night long the seven remaining men of the posse stayed to see Sonny die. But he did not die, and shortly after dawn the sheriff rode off for Chollaville, leaving one of his men behind.

"If he doesn't cash in today, he'll do it tomorrow," was his opinion. "Queer how he hangs on. Send me word when it's over."

But two more days passed, and then several more. Sonny Tabor lived. The crisis past, he began to mend rapidly. Ma's nursing and tender care had pulled him through.

When the sheriff found that Sonny was going to get well,

he asked if Stewart would be responsible for him until he was able to be removed to the jail at Chollaville. Stewart consented. It seemed that Sonny would live to hang, after all.

Sonny had grown to love Ma, and worship her. She was his angel. And she, too, found that she cared for the young outlaw more than she would admit. He looked so harmless, so innocent of any crime, with his boyish, smiling face and frank eyes.

"Tell me about yourself, Sonny," Ma asked him one day when the lad was able to sit up.

"Isn't much to tell about me, Ma," he said slowly. "There's a lot of things, of course, that I'm sorry for."

"And that you're ashamed of?" she questioned softly.

"No, ma'am," he told her half defiantly.

"Is it true that you've killed ten men, a . . . a dozen, with the ones that were shot in your last fight?"

His face instantly became earnest. "Yes, Ma," he said. "I guess it is. I'm sorry that it has to be, but it's the truth. I had to kill in order to live. A price on my head. Every head turned against me, and every man my enemy. Why, I even slept with a gun in my hand. It's a hard country, Ma. If I've killed, it's been in self-defense, always. I've never stolen."

"Oh, how glad I am to hear that," she said, as if a weight had been taken from her mind. "You poor boy. When they told me you were bad, I just couldn't believe it. I know what treatment an outlaw gets. But, Sonny, what started you to be an outlaw?"

"I killed a man," Sonny confessed in a hushed voice. "I shot a man when I was a kid . . . about fourteen years old. It was this way, Ma. I didn't have any folks, any mother like you, or maybe it wouldn't have happened. I had to shine boots for a living . . . had to drift from saloon to saloon.

Well, one day a man tried to make me take a drink."

"And what did you do?" Ma demanded with interest.

"He had a quirt and began beating me with it when I wouldn't do as he said. A man I knew tried to help me, and this drunken fellow drew a knife on him and would've killed him, if I hadn't run behind the bar and picked up a gun that was there. I shot him."

"And then?"

"Well, since then I've been on the run, a hunted man. But I want you to believe me, Ma . . . you've been just like a ma to me . . . when I say that I've never killed for money, or to rob."

"I do, Sonny, I do," Ma assured.

From that time on, Ma and Sonny were even closer to each other. She cared for him as she would a son, and he loved her like a mother. Ed Stewart was angry and uneasy. He hated Sonny, but until now he had said nothing for his wife's sake. But the time had come, he decided, for a show-down. Ma must know.

So one morning he called her outside for a private talk and told her. She turned white at first and seemed to be on the point of collapse. Awkwardly Ed tried to soothe her.

"Never you mind, honey," he said. "We'll have him out o' here in short order. He's sure to be moved now, and I'll send word to the sheriff to come and take him. He'll be punished well for Bob's murder, I'll guarantee. They'll string him up in Chollaville, first thing."

"But, Ed," she sobbed, "I can't! I can't! Sonny isn't the man to shoot another down for robbery. I won't believe it!"

To her husband's disgust, she went inside the sick room and put the question to Sonny himself. The moment he saw her, he knew something was wrong. Her eyes were swollen from weeping, and it was all she could do to speak.

"Sonny," she asked finally, "did you kill my son, Bob Stewart?"

The question made him flinch with pain and surprise. But he shook his head.

"Think!" she urged. On Hacha Hill! They say you buried him there and made off with the gold he was carrying from Chollaville."

"I didn't, Ma," he said piteously, "I didn't. It hurts me to think that you might not believe me, but it's true. I don't know anything about it."

For a long time, she looked into his open blue eyes. Then she sighed, dried her eyes, and said to him: "Sonny, I believe you. I don't know why I do, but I do."

That night Sheriff Nowell and his posse came to take Sonny to jail in Chollaville.

VI

With Sonny gone, Ma Stewart's life seemed barren and empty. She believed in his innocence with a faith that only a woman and a mother can have. She had pleaded long with Sheriff Nowell, asking him not to take Sonny, or at least not so soon. But to her pleas, the law—grim and relentless— had turned a deaf ear.

Ed Stewart couldn't quite understand Ma, even though he had lived happily with her for many years. It seemed unbelievable to him that she could care for this Sonny Tabor—this desperado who had killed and robbed Bob Stewart, their son. The facts in the case were, to him, ironclad. Sonny Tabor was without a doubt guilty of murder and banditry.

Ross, the Triangle Cross foreman, was the most bitter in

his tirades against Sonny. He swore about him daily. The other riders also believed that Sonny had killed Bob Stewart. There seemed nothing else to believe. Besides, wasn't Tabor an outlaw with a long record?

A possible exception was Moffitt. Ma confided more in him than in anyone else, now that her husband was against her. Moffitt listened and was troubled. He didn't exactly know what to believe. Somehow he had liked Tabor and admired him.

In the meantime, Sonny was in the jail in Chollaville, awaiting execution. The hanging was set for the following week, and then postponed, as the young outlaw had had a relapse from his wounds. Days passed and still Tabor remained unhanged. Ma Stewart rejoiced. Ed Stewart fidgeted.

The truth of the matter was Sonny had more friends than he thought. His bravery, his boyish freedom from any guile, had excited the admiration of many. Eventually, of course, he would be hanged, but there were many delays.

Day by day, the old ranchman of the Triangle Cross grew more angry and dissatisfied with the way things were going. He wanted to see the murder of his boy avenged, and as quickly as possible.

Ross, too, inflamed him with hints and suggestions. Why, the foreman, would demand, didn't somebody *do* something? In a case of this kind, there is but one remedy in the West. If the law wouldn't do it, Ross said, it was time someone else did. "He ought ter be taken out o' that jail and strung up, if you ask me," he snarled.

"We'll wait a few days," Stewart replied, with a gleam in his old eagle eyes.

A few days passed, and Sonny was still in jail, with the hanging postponed for another week. The sheriff, it seemed, was out of town on business and could not attend to the execution.

It was then that Stewart completely lost patience. Gathering his men together after dinner, he made his plans.

"Ross has been right," he told them. "It's time we did something. After nightfall tonight we'll ride into Chollaville and give Tabor the punishment he deserves."

Moffitt was worried. The youth was torn between his duty to his employer and his love for Ma Stewart. Besides, the idea of lynching Sonny Tabor was repugnant to him. After thinking it over carefully, he took Ma to one side and told her in a whisper what was in the wind.

Ma Stewart was heartbroken at first, and then furious. "Oh, I wish I was a man!" she exclaimed. "I didn't think that Ed would plan such a thing. And Ross. I never liked or understood that man. What shall I do?"

"Well, Ma," Moffitt returned, "if there's anything I can do, I'm plumb willin'."

"You mean that?"

"Of course I do, Ma."

"And you don't think that Sonny killed Bob?"

"Somehow I don't," Moffitt said thoughtfully. "Sonny isn't the man to boast of his shootings. Some bandits might, but he isn't the kind that would do it. That message in the empty cartridge looked queer to me from the first."

"Well, then," asked Ma breathlessly, "will you help me save him?"

Moffitt didn't hesitate. "Sure I will. But how?"

Taking care that they would not be heard, Ma suggested a way, and they planned a rescue together. Moffitt was to sprain his ankle, or pretend to do so, and this would excuse him from accompanying the other men. Ma knew of a short cut that might be made with a buckboard, and by driving hard they could easily reach Chollaville before Ed Stewart, since the lynching party, with the whole night before them, would be in no hurry.

All went well. Moffitt, late that day, faked a fall from a young horse he was breaking, and he did it so well that he aroused the suspicions of nobody. The other men ate a hasty supper and at twilight prepared for their journey. Ma asked where they were going, but, of course, she took pains not to be too curious.

"Just ridin' into Chollaville for the evenin'," explained Ed evasively. "Bein' as young Moffitt's hurt, I guess he'll have to stay with you. So you won't be lonesome. Good bye."

"Good bye!" called Ma Stewart cheerfully. And she concealed a smile.

The Triangle Cross men left the ranch at an easy walk, easing their horses along and evidently in very good humor. No sooner were they out of sight when Ma called after Moffitt. It was time to act.

The cowpuncher already had the buckboard ready, and Ma smuggled out an extra .45 revolver and a belt from the house. In the blacksmith shop Moffitt found a good, heavy file, and they added this to the tools of the evening.

In a jiffy they were racing through the short cut in the half darkness to Chollaville. If the buckboard would only hold together, all would be well.

VII

The night was bright with moonlight. Like a big yellow lantern, the Arizona moon hung low over the horizon, making the wide sweeps of the desert nearly as light as day. The few citizens of the little town of Chollaville were, for the most part, fast asleep. The night owls were uptown on crooked Main Street, drinking in the saloons. The scattered adobe section where the town jail sprawled was deserted and at peace.

Sonny Tabor was staring out of the small grated window, lost in thought and looking at the dim lands of the valley that he would in all probability never ride again. Something was on his mind, something puzzling. That anyone should even suspect him of deliberate murder and robbery, in spite of his outlaw career, hurt him, and that his supposed victim should be Ma Stewart's son hurt him still more.

What had she said? Hacha Hill? He knew something about that hill—something out of the ordinary that he had seen there. But what was it? In vain he searched his memory. Since the sickness that had followed his wounding, part of his life seemed a blank. But one thing he did know—he had not robbed and killed Bob Stewart.

Life's a funny thing, he mused. *Someone did shoot young Stewart down. But who?* There seemed to be no use in worrying his aching head about it, but although he tried to dismiss it from his mind, he found that he could not.

From time to time, he heard his guard's feet scraping in the outer part of the jail. Except for that, and the faint sound of drunken singing from a distant saloon, the silence was unbroken.

The jail office door was thrown open for comfort, and it was at the doorway that the guard—Sonny's jailer—spent most of his time. He was a thin-faced, sleepy-eyed deputy, and he passed the time smoking cigarettes and whistling to himself.

Suddenly the guard heard a sound exactly like a muffled

footfall in soft sand. His low whistle ceased, and he jumped for the door, hand on his gun.

"Put 'em up high," ordered a steady voice.

The guard's right eye was so close to the ugly .45 revolver muzzle that he imagined he could see the bullet on the way out. With a startled grunt, he took his hand off his gun butt and elevated it to join its mate. Both arms aloft and mouth sagging open, he looked the picture of helplessness.

"That's right," commanded the man's voice again. "Now lie down while I tie you. One word out o' you, and there's liable to be lead flyin' your way, because my trigger finger's got the Saint Vitus dance."

While he was being bound and gagged, the guard obtained a good look at his captors. One was a determined-looking young man. The other was a woman.

"Guess we won't need the file," the youth said while searching the guard's pockets. "Here's his keys to the jail."

Then, leaving their prisoner flat on his face and securely bound, they approached the iron door that opened into Sonny's cell.

When Sonny Tabor heard a key grate in the lock, he imagined that it was only his jailer, although what the man could want in his cell at that hour was more than he could fathom. He was amazed when he turned his head and saw two familiar faces staring at him through the gloom.

"Sonny!" Ma Stewart called.

The young outlaw's eyes opened wide.

"Why, what are you doin' here, Ma?"

In a voice trembling with anxiety, she told him. "And they'll be here any minute," she finished. "Here, take this gun. Promise me just one thing . . . that you won't fire on my husband."

"Of course not, Ma," he said gently, "nor upon anyone else, unless absolutely necessary."

"You can take one of the horses from the buckboard," Ma explained. "There's a saddle in it, too. But you must hurry."

"Strike for the border, Tabor," Moffitt advised. "I'm sure wishin' you luck."

Sonny wrung Moffitt's hand. Then he buckled on the gun belt, with a sigh of relief. He had never thought to feel the comforting weight of a .45 on his hip again.

The three of them opened the cell door and started cautiously for the outer portion of the jail. Moffitt was in the lead, and he was about to open the door when a voice rang out:

"Stick up your hands!" It was the voice of Sheriff Nowell.

Instead of obeying the command, Moffitt leaped suddenly backward, nearly bowling over Sonny and Ma Stewart.

A bullet flattened and glanced against the iron cell door as they leaped inside and closed it behind them.

"There's three or four men with him! I saw 'em in the moonlight!" Moffitt cried. "We're trapped!"

VIII

In the outer room they heard the swift trampling of feet and the sound of men's excited voices. Among them they recognized the guard's. Evidently they had freed him, and he was telling his story.

The future now looked black, indeed. The sheriff had blundered up, by accident, more than likely, to spoil all their carefully laid plans.

"Come out o' there, one at a time," they heard Nowell shout, "or we'll bring you out!"

Then they heard him giving swift orders. His men were to get help and fetch something to batter down the iron door.

What was to be done? It was Ma who made the suggestion that was to squeeze them from a tight situation. "It's a good thing we brought the file, after all," she whispered.

Sonny examined the bars of the window on the other side of the cell. Luckily they were not very heavy and were somewhat eaten with red rust. Taking the file, he went to work with all his strength.

The sheriff's men were making so much noise on their side of the big adobe building that they could not hear the steady *rasp-rasp-rasp* that Sonny was making as he sawed at one of the bars. They were striking the cell door with thundering blows—blows that shook the building to its foundation. They were using a heavy timber for a battering ram, and every charge they made threatened to tear the door from its massive hinges.

Suddenly the bar Sonny was filing gave way. He had succeeded more quickly than he had hoped. But there was still more work to do. Getting Moffitt to help him, they used the cut bar for a lever and succeeded in bending the other bars out of the way, leaving a sizable hole.

Moffitt was the first through, and Ma was next with the two men, one inside the prison and one out, helping her. Sonny Tabor was last. As he swung himself halfway to freedom, he heard the sudden shuffling of many boots in the sand. They had been discovered! The sheriff's posse had at last found out that there was something amiss in the vicinity of the jail window.

As Sonny dropped to the ground, he drew his gun. "I'm

Sonny Tabor," he shouted, "and I'm armed!"

His words took effect instantly. Everyone scurried for cover like jack rabbits. Brave as the posse was, they had learned their lesson at the Triangle Cross. When Sonny Tabor was on the warpath and armed with the tools of war, it meant that somebody would get hurt.

The only man who had any idea at all of shooting it out with Sonny was Sheriff Nowell. When Sonny punctured his hat with a .45 bullet as a pointed warning, Nowell took it, deciding that it was foolish to make a target out of himself in the bright moonlight. He quickly ducked behind the building.

"The buckboard!" Sonny heard Moffitt cry. "Follow us!"

Tabor had never believed that Ma Stewart could be so spry. It was all he could do to keep up with her and Moffitt as they made for the shadows of the gloomy paloverdes in the shallow arroyo, where the trail forked three ways into the desert.

Revolver shots were ringing out behind them now, but they might as well have been aimed at the moon, for all the damage they did.

The two men helped Ma Stewart into the buckboard, and in a flash they were off, cutting across the desert like mad. The soft sand muffled the wheels, and the vehicle made little noise as it sped toward the mountains. It swayed this way and that as the horses swung about to avoid the mesquites and cactus.

Moffitt chuckled, after five minutes had passed. "I guess we done it."

Ma was whipping the horses and hanging on. In the moonlight Sonny could see her face. She was smiling broadly, and there was a twinkle in her kindly eyes.

"I'd like to see Ed's face"—she laughed—"when he gets to Chollaville."

They were to see Ed's face—and soon. Sonny's eyes were on something far away, and suddenly he lay his hand on Ma Stewart's arm.

"Riders!" he exclaimed. "Stop the buckboard and pull off the trail a little, before they hear us."

"That can't be the sheriff and his posse," Moffitt muttered as he made out the approaching figures out from the moonlit background.

"No, those are the Triangle Cross men," Sonny declared. "They're just gettin' here."

One side of the trail was bordered by a low thicket of paloverde trees. Sonny leaped out. Guiding the horses, he soon had the buckboard and the team hidden from sight of anyone following the trail into town.

There was the chance, too, that the pursuit from Chollaville would ride up from the other direction at any moment. It was a tight situation, and it was just a question of whether luck would be with them.

Moffitt drew his Colt.

"No shootin', old pal." Sonny smiled at him. "If they see us, why I'll give myself up, that's all. I don't want any killin' on account o' me."

Scarcely breathing, the three of them waited in the paloverde thicket. They were out of sight, and, as soon as Ed Stewart and his men passed, they could take to the trail again.

Gradually the five horsemen drew nearer, Ed Stewart and Ross, the foreman, in the lead, coming along at an easy pace. The moon shone on their faces, outlining every line and expression. Sonny's eyes were narrowing.

When the horsemen were almost opposite, he gripped

Ma's arm and whispered: "Who is that man riding with your husband?"

"Ross," she breathed.

It was the first time Sonny Tabor had seen the Triangle Cross foreman at close range. Glints of steel appeared in his watching eyes. Memory was coming back to him. What was it Ma had said about Hacha Hill? Why did he link Ross's lean, hard face with that hill? There was a connection somewhere.

"Sonny," Ma gasped in a horrified voice, "what are you going to do?"

The young outlaw, gun in hand, was stepping directly in front of the Triangle Cross outfit as they approached on the Chollaville trail.

IX

Leaving Ma Stewart and Moffitt, both amazed and horrified, behind him in the cover of the paloverde, Sonny Tabor acted with the swiftness of a desperate wolf.

"Put 'em up!" he barked, and his voice was as metallic as the sound of a cocked gun hammer.

The Triangle Cross men were not cowards, but Sonny had the drop. His menacing gun muzzle seemed to be on every man alike. One by one, they put up their hands. Stewart was the last to do so.

The thing had happened so suddenly and so unexpectedly that they were overcome with astonishment. Sonny Tabor, the man they had come to hang! Under any other circumstances, the startled expressions of their faces would have been comical.

Even after the first surprise was over, they dared not

make a move to draw their guns. Sonny Tabor had a reputation. He could shoot as quickly as the bat of an eyelash.

"Gents, I thank you," Sonny said sweetly.

There was no sound save the heavy breathing of the men
and a few low oaths from Ross.

"I didn't intend to bother you," Sonny went on, "but I
changed my mind. Moffitt," he called sharply, "will you
come out and relieve these *hombres* o' their guns?"

Moffitt, almost as astonished-looking as the others,
slipped out of his hiding place, followed at a short distance
by Ma Stewart.

At the sight of his wife, Ed's jaw dropped.

"You . . . here," he groaned. "What's the world comin'
to?"

"You'd be surprised, Edward J. Stewart," Ma replied
warmly.

She helped Moffitt gather the guns of the five captured
riders. They were tossed into the buckboard.

Stewart's eyes were blazing as he turned them on
Moffitt. "Your sprained ankle healed up quick," he said sar-
castically. "You're not only fired, but I'll have you run out
of the county for this."

When the prisoners were all disarmed, Sonny stepped up
face to face with the old ranchman. "Mister Stewart," he
said, "wasn't your son Bob killed at Hacha Hill?"

"You know blamed well he was, you coyote!" jerked out
Stewart, his face distorted with wrath. "It's a good thing I
can't get my hands on your throat, you killer!"

Sonny smiled faintly. "No doubt of it," he said. "But
would you mind lettin' me see what you found on that
grave up there? Moffitt told me about it, and I'm plumb et
up with curiosity."

Ross snarled out something, and Sonny turned his

flashing eyes on him. "If you don't stop that cussin' when there's a lady present," he said quietly, "I'll stop you in a way you won't like."

Ross shut up.

Stewart, grumbling, decided to obey Sonny's request. Reaching in his vest pocket, he took out the cartridge and handed it to Tabor.

Tabor shook out the note, read it by the light of the moon, and smiled quizzically at Stewart.

"I don't smoke cigarettes," he said. "Queer that I'd carry a supply o' papers just to write epitaphs on, ain't it?"

Stewart sneered. "How do I know what you do or don't do?" he grunted.

"You don't," said Sonny pleasantly, and then continued: "This cartridge is Forty-One caliber."

"Huh!" Stewart exclaimed, startled. "Let's see! I didn't notice that."

Sonny handed it to him, and he examined it curiously.

"I use Forty-Fives." Sonny grinned. "Always."

"There ain't so many Forty-Ones owned hereabouts," said the old ranchman thoughtfully.

"There's quite a few," put in Ross quickly. "I own a Forty-One myself."

"I'd thought o' that," said Stewart quietly.

"Stewart," snapped Sonny, "I want to know where this man was the day your son was killed." He pointed directly at Ross.

The foreman's face grew suddenly evil. With teeth bared, he glared at Sonny. "I was in Dry Springs that day," he snarled.

"Or supposed to be." It was Moffitt who spoke up suddenly. "You weren't at the ranch till night."

"On April Eleventh," Sonny drawled, "I happened to pass by Hacha Hill. . . ."

"Of course you did!" barked Ross, who felt the coils tightening about him. "And you robbed and killed Bob Stewart."

"Shut up," warned Sonny dangerously. "Ross, I saw *you* at the foot o' Hacha Hill. You had hidden something . . . buried it in the sand. I saw you smoothin' the ground over with your boot. Your hoss was tied nearby."

"You lie!"

"I don't lie. I saw you, but thought nothin' of it at the time. I was a hunted man and didn't dare show myself. I rode past you through a mesquite thicket and on out o' sight."

Stewart's face was a study. A triumphant look was in Ma's eyes.

From the direction of Chollaville came the faint sound of drumming hoofs.

Sonny heard it and smiled. "Reckon that's the sheriff after me." He turned to Stewart. "Care to ride to Hacha Hill tonight and see what's buried under a certain giant cactus? I've got to dodge this posse, and that will be as good a direction for me to ride as any."

"Don't listen to his lies, Ed!" Ross almost screamed. "I been workin' for you over a year. I never. . . ."

"Workin'." Sonny smiled. "I call it layin' low. You're wanted in Pima County right now for murder. I know you. You're right name's Jack Demming."

It took Stewart but an instant to decide. "We'll ride with you, Tabor, to Hacha Hill," he said.

Sonny paused to listen again. The approaching hoofs were still far off.

"*Bueno,*" he drawled, "and to show you that I'm in good

faith, I'll give you back your guns. Fetch 'em, Moffitt. And saddle me one of the hosses from the buckboard." Moffitt went to do it. "I'm not makin' any exception o' you, Ross," he said. "Here's yours."

"I'll promise you they won't be used," Stewart declared. "At least, not until we've got to the bottom o' this."

Sonny left Moffitt to take charge of Ma and see her home safely to the ranch.

"Good bye," Tabor told her, trying to keep his voice steady. "I want you to know that I'll always carry your memory in my heart. I can't ever thank you, but someday we might meet again. I'll be a better man for havin' met you. From now on, if they'll let me, I'll be an honest citizen. *Adiós*."

"Good bye, Sonny," Ma said. "You'll always be with me in my prayers. *Adiós*."

And with a rattle, the buckboard drawn by the remaining horse was gone.

The horsemen from Chollaville were about 200 yards away.

"Now gents," said Sonny, turning to the Triangle Cross outfit, "I reckon we'll be movin', *pronto!*"

X

Striking off to the southward at top speed, Sonny, accompanied by Stewart and his men, soon outdistanced the sheriff's quickly gathered posse. It was doubtful if Nowell even saw them, for they took the course of a dry arroyo for some distance before coming up into the desert again.

Stewart's mind was in a turmoil. Somehow he couldn't help but believe that there was truth in what Sonny Tabor had said. The young outlaw had more than shown his sincerity by allowing them all, even Ross, to have their guns again.

Stewart was keeping his eyes on Ross, and he saw to it that the foreman rode in the middle of the party, so that he could not escape. Now that Sonny had opened his eyes, certain dark suspicions were forming in the old ranchman's mind. Ross was the only one who knew, with the exception of Stewart himself, that Bob was carrying the payroll that fateful day in April.

Besides, Ed said to himself, *Ma believed in Sonny . . . and, by gosh, she's always right!*

Ross's face was white. He saw that he was being watched by every member of the outfit, and he was trembling inwardly. And only he knew what they would find at the foot of the giant cactus by Hacha Hill. His hand itched for his Colt, but Sonny's eyes were always on him, as keen as a gimlet.

Mile after mile disappeared beneath their ponies' drumming hoofs. Hills began to loom up before them, outlined in the moonlight. Presently, after they had followed a dry creek for several miles, they saw the Hacha, sinister and ugly.

"We're nearly there, boys," Stewart grunted.

Scattered around the foot of the mound of volcanic rock were several giant cacti. But only one of them was branched. Sonny pointed to where it stood in the moonlight, lifting a solitary branch toward the starry vault overhead.

"That's it," Tabor said. "That's where I saw Ross diggin'."

All dismounted. The foreman was swearing under his breath, and his eyes glistened in the moonlight. The crisis was at hand. He shook visibly, his nerve breaking.

"Ed Stewart," he murmured, "I . . . I swear I don't know anything about this."

"You swear too damned much," Ed said shortly. "Frank," he told one of his cowpunchers, "dig under that cactus and see what you find."

"On the west side," Sonny suggested.

While the cowpuncher dug, using his big hunting knife, Stewart cast a glance up at the hill above. His son was up there. Would he be avenged? He wished more than ever that he knew the answer to it all.

Already the cowman had made a sizable hole. Suddenly his knife struck something that sounded like tin. All of them gathered closer around, almost holding their breaths in their intense interest.

"A tin can," someone said.

"And plenty heavy," Frank grunted, as he fished it out with difficulty. "Why . . . why, it's full o' gold."

He had bent back the lid, and the mellow light of the moon fell upon something bright and yellow. Money. Gold pieces.

"That's the payroll cash, all right," Stewart muttered thickly. "And I guess if Sonny had put it there, he wouldn't have brought us here to give it back."

It was then that Ross made his last desperate move. Leaping a step backward, his right paw went down to the butt of his revolver—and it traveled fast.

"Heads up!" Stewart yelled.

But Sonny's head had been up all the time. His hand moved also and it moved even quicker than Ross's. Flame blazed from Sonny Tabor's hip. Ross tottered on his feet, then sat down suddenly. Lead had nipped him, and nipped him mortally, for he released his hold on his gun and began to gasp. With glazing eyes he stared up at the little half circle of men.

"Guess . . . I . . . overplayed my . . . hand." He grinned faintly, gamer now in death than he had been while living. "Come closer . . . Stewart."

The old rancher bent over him.

"I deserve . . . this," Ross muttered. "It was me that got . . . Bob, all right. I'm . . . sorry I laid . . . the blame . . . on Tabor. I hid the gold . . . expected . . . to get it when . . . everything blew . . . over." His voice suddenly choked and grew weaker. "I'm fallin' . . . through the dark . . . the dark. . . ."

He dropped backward into the sand and moved no more.

For a long time there was silence. Then Stewart sighed. He turned to Sonny, held out his hand and said: "Well, I guess the mystery is settled, Sonny Tabor. I can't thank you, and I'll never forget you. You've been a man, and I want you to forgive me for what I thought. Ed Stewart's just a plumb born fool . . . even if he has got a girl like Ma for a wife. What's on your program now? If there's anything I can do . . . ?"

Sonny gripped the old rancher's hand, smiled, and shook his head.

"No, I'm strikin' for the border," he replied. "There's a promise I made to Ma, and I'm goin' to keep it. Reckon there's nothin' you can do for me, for I'm still outside the law. But if you don't mind, do it for young Moffitt. He helped a lot."

"He'll be my next foreman." Stewart chuckled. "Any other message for Ma, Sonny?"

"Nothin' . . . only . . . well, tell her I'll send for her the next time I get in jail."

And smiling boyishly, Sonny swung himself into his saddle. With a wave of his big Stetson in the moonlight, and in time to the jingling of spurs, he headed at a hot pace toward dim Sonora.

Sonny Tabor's Gun School

Originally published in *Wild West Weekly* in the November 1, 1930 issue, this story goes from a hangman's tree to a cattle ranch to a schoolhouse where Sonny finds himself being assisted by none other than a smart-aleck nine-year old. It was one of the five stories that comprised *Wanted— Sonny Tabor* published by Chelsea House in 1931. For its appearance here those parts of the story, not included in the Chelsea House compilation, have been restored.

I

It was almost morning, but the sky was unlighted by any stars, and there was no moon. The tiny fire, glowing redly against the jet shadows of the Azul Mountains, made a brave attempt to conquer the gloom, but failed. Its flickering light, in that vast wilderness of mesa and valley, upland and desert, seemed no more important than a firefly's gleam. The campfire, however, was hidden with some care. It could be seen only from one direction, and unless one smelled the pungent odor of the burning mesquite wood, he could be likely to ride by it unawares. A youth of twenty was warming his hands at the blaze, and at the edge of the creeping shadows, a paint pony waited, saddled and ready.

"I don't know what woke me up, Paint," he murmured, as if trying to cheer himself by speaking aloud. "But somethin' did." He looked at the sky and added a little more fuel to the blaze. "It's a queer night. You shore miss the stars in Arizona when they don't shine."

The night was cold. It lacked less than an hour until dawn and a chill wind was singing through the greasewood. There was no sound, not even the far-off yap of a prowling coyote. The ruddy light of the glowing embers outlined his lithe, trim figure. He was crouching, and so low swung were his two Colt .45s that the tips of the worn leather holsters nearly touched the ground. A cream-colored Stetson almost, but not quite, hid his features. They were regular and boyish. The clean-cut mouth was frank and pleasing, especially when he was smiling, and that was most of the time. His blue eyes had an innocent look, making him appear even younger than he was. A closer glance, though, would have noted other things in those eyes—a certain wild courage that was more than just recklessness. Experience was there, too, and a strange sadness of the sort one sees in the eyes of a haunted animal. The slight mark on one cheek was not a dimple but the scar left by a .45-caliber bullet. It was Sonny Tabor, the most sought outlaw in Arizona, a wanted man who had killed a man for every year of his life, according to rumor—and rumor in the Southwest is usually correct.

Suddenly the paint pony lay back its ears. At the same instant, Sonny Tabor heard a cautious crunch of footsteps in the sand. In a breath, he had jumped away from the glow of the fire, his two guns out of their holsters and leveled at a slowly moving black hulk in the darkness.

"You're quick on the pull, kid!" exclaimed a deep and throaty voice. "But put up your hardware. I'm on the dodge, and the law's after me . . . the same as you."

A stooped, broad-chested man came into the ring of firelight. He was hatless and disheveled, and dragged his feet with weariness. He was holding his bony hands palm out-

ward to show that they held no weapon. Sonny, examining
him attentively, put his guns away.

"What makes you think," he drawled, "that the law
wants me?"

The stranger's bushy eyebrows went up, and he
shrugged expressively. "Does an honest *hombre* build a fire
in a barranca at three-thirty in the mornin'? And does he
pack two quick-draw guns like yours, kid? My name's
Shaw . . . Jed Shaw."

This newcomer seemed friendly enough, but Tabor
hardly liked his looks. His whiskery, soiled face was coarse
and bestial. The eyes of this desperado, too, were calcu-
lating and beady as they roamed over Tabor's little camp,
missing nothing.

"You're welcome to share my fire," Sonny said shortly.

"Didn't catch your name, kid."

"I didn't give it."

"Have it your own way. What's a name, anyways?"
grunted Shaw after a pause. "Ain't got a drink, have you?"

"I don't drink."

"Got the makin's?" persisted the other.

"I don't smoke, either. Sorry," said Sonny Tabor briefly.

"What *do* you do?" grumbled the stranger in an irritated
tone. "You must be a sho' enough baby."

"I shoot," replied Sonny, "when I have to. Reckon that's
my one real bad habit. I hope I'm not curious, but where
did you come from?"

Shaw spat into the fire and grinned. "Ever hear o' King
Johnny's gang? Reckon you have, huh?"

"I've heard plenty," admitted Sonny Tabor with a quick
glint in his blue eyes.

"Well, I'm one of 'em," went on Shaw confidentially. He
took a seat by the fire and looked across at the young

outlaw. "We pulled a job yesterday, and Sheriff Quinn chased us with a posse. My hoss was shot from under me, and I got cut off. The rest o' the boys escaped without much trouble, but I had a hell of a time makin' my getaway on foot. They've been after me most of the night."

"There's not a posse on your heels now, I hope," Sonny remarked softly.

"What's the matter, kid?" Shaw grinned, opening a cavernous mouth. "You afraid?"

"Not exactly," replied Sonny Tabor quietly.

"Well, you don't need to worry. I shook 'em off hours ago." Shaw chuckled. "I'll get in touch with the gang tomorra. OK. By the way, kid . . . whatever your name is . . . why don't you join up with King Johnny? Why, we make big killin's. Lots o' *dinero*. Why be a lone wolf and be content with small pickin's?"

"From what I've heard," drawled Sonny, "you're a gang of cold killers."

Shaw took this as a compliment. "Heh-heh. We got the whole territory scared, all right." He laughed. "King Johnny, by the way, is one o' the fastest gunmen I ever seen. He's only about five years older'n you, but he's the toughest man in Arizony. They say thet outlaw, Sonny Tabor, is good with guns, but I'd put King Johnny up against Tabor any day."

Sonny looked at Shaw closely and decided that Shaw did not even guess he was talking to Sonny Tabor himself. He smiled. "I've heard it said somewhere," murmured the young outlaw, "that this Tabor tries to go straight. I heard that he was forced outside the law when he was just a boy o' fourteen, and that he's never robbed any one."

"Huh," sneered Shaw, "you talk as if you knowed more about Tabor than I do."

"You know him well?" Sonny asked, amused.

"Well, I've never seen him, but I know all about him. Don't fool yourself . . . he's as bad as any of us. And if he don't steal, how does he live? Him honest? Don't make me laugh, kid."

Sonny made no reply, but a spot of color had appeared on his rounded, tanned cheeks.

The burly desperado talked on: "I want to tell you about thet job we pulled off yesterday. Leave it to King Johnny to smell out the *dinero*. There was a rancher on the Bonita . . . *hombre* named Ferris. We got wind of four thousand bucks he had hid in the house. We got it."

"I'd rather not hear of your dirty doin's," Sonny said grimly.

But Shaw went on, as if he hadn't heard. His throaty voice was boastful and exulting: "There was 'bout half a dozen people on the ranch, all told. King Johnny killed Ferris hisself. We wiped 'em all out. One was a woman. We'd have let her alone, if she hadn't grabbed a Winchester. I had to. . . ."

"You killed a woman?" demanded Sonny Tabor. His eyes had become hard, blue lights. They were not mild and innocent now.

"What of it? I had to do it, or. . . ."

"Reach for your gun!" Sonny cried.

The bullet scar on his cheek no longer looked like a dimple. His voice rang like the beat of iron on steel. Shaw's face went blank with amazement. Slowly he took a step backward, then another. Something in Sonny's expression frightened him.

"I'm out o' ammunition," he mumbled. "Don't . . . start anything. What in blazes is eatin' you, kid? I. . . ."

"You lie. Your gun's loaded," Sonny Tabor snapped. "I

never saw a murderer yet that wasn't a coward at the show-down." He unbuckled his guns and tossed them to one side. "We'll have it this way, then."

Now that Sonny had disarmed himself, Shaw's expression changed. Rage and fury gleamed in his shifty eyes. He bared tobacco-stained teeth in a snarl of defiance. "Here's whar I beat your head into the ground, you little whelp," he grated.

It looked as if he could do it. He was about thirty pounds heavier than Sonny, and his arms and hairy chest bulged with muscle. He rushed. Powerful blows, aimed at Sonny's face, went left and right. If any of them had connected, it would have gone hard with the youthful outlaw. Sonny, however, eluded the charge. He was astonishingly quick on his feet. He came at Shaw at a bound, ducked under a sledge-hammer blow, and lashed out at the desperado's mouth. Shaw went rolling over and over, dazed and half stunned. The blow, with Sonny's trail-hardened muscles behind it, had been like the kick of a mule. And it had landed scientifically, perfectly timed and placed.

Shaw shook the hair out of his eyes, raised himself up on one hand, and reached for his gun with the other. "I'll kill you," he panted.

But Sonny dived at him. Steel fingers closed over the desperado's wrist, and both men began struggling for the weapon.

Dawn was breaking. The Azul Mountains were already pink against the sky, and nearby objects became visible. The fire was almost out.

In the scuffle for life, neither man observed the strange actions of Paint. The animal tossed his well-shaped head and moved his ears attentively. He seemed nervous and anxious. Sonny was twisting Shaw's wrist. Beads of sweat stood out on the ruffian's distorted face. They were breathing heavily. Then, just as the revolver dropped to the sand, a voice rang out from beyond the fire.

"Stick 'em up! We got you covered!"

Six horsemen, holding leveled Colts, were outlined in the faint light of the early morning. It was the law.

Shaw rolled free from Sonny's grip and thrust up his arms. Sonny, after a quiet survey of the situation, did likewise. Shaw's face was drawn and tortured with fear, but Sonny only smiled resignedly.

"Well," chuckled one of the six riders, "this is better than we looked for. We was chasin' one of 'em, and found two. Tie their hands, boys. Put 'em both on that paint pony."

Sonny understood. The posse took him for a member of the King Johnny gang of border cut-throats. Shaw had been trailed to Sonny's hiding place through a strange prank of fate. Sonny would never have been caught alone.

The desperado was swearing under his breath as they bound him—more to keep up his courage than for any other reason, for his coarse face was drawn with fear. His thick lips quivered. "This is your fault, kid," he whined.

Sonny, although he thought differently, said nothing. One of the riders picked up his guns, and three others bound his wrists so tightly that the rope cut into his flesh. Then he and Shaw were placed on Paint, and the little cavalcade moved on through the mesquites down into the valley of the Azul.

"What your name?" snapped the man who seemed to be in command of the posse, although his badge read DEPUTY instead of SHERIFF. He glared into the big desperado's chalky face.

"Shaw . . . Jed Shaw," replied the bandit. "Honest, officers, I never had nothin' to do with. . . ."

"Don't lie to us." The deputy laughed harshly. "You're the same *hombre* we chased all day yesterday. We ain't blind. What's your name, kid?" he demanded, looking at Sonny Tabor.

"Mister Ex Wyzee," drawled Sonny quietly.

"Don't want to talk, eh?" growled one of the other riders. "Mebbe he'll change his tune in a few minutes. What about stringin' these *hombres* up right now?"

"Mebbe we better wait for Sheriff Quinn. He said he'd meet us down on the river," spoke up another.

"What's the use of waitin'?" said the first speaker. "Thar's a big cottonwood down below you. We'll string 'em up."

"*Bueno.*"

As they rode slowly down through the alders on the dry riverbank, Sonny's mind was busy, weighing his chances. No matter how dark the situation, he never gave up all hope. This time, though, he was in a deep hole. Certain death faced him. What if he did try to convince these men that he was not a party to the Ferris murders, not a member of King Johnny's gang? He knew that it would make no difference at all. For Sonny Tabor, too, had a death sentence—although an unjust one—hanging over his head. They'd hang him just as quickly—probably more quickly—if they knew who he really was.

It was quite light now. Sonny could see the mountains towering on both sides of the riverbed, the green of the trees that fringed it, and the colorful sands under the hoofs of the ponies. Somewhere down below, a bird—a yellow warbler—burst into song to greet the morning. It was hard to believe that death in its most terrible form awaited them, that their minutes were numbered, and that soon two lifeless forms would be swinging drearily at the end of a rope.

Shaw was shaking from head to foot. His teeth chattered. In spite of his contempt for the man, and in spite of the fact that Shaw certainly deserved hanging, Sonny was sorry for him.

The lynching party drew rein under the big cottonwood tree. They dismounted.

"Oh, my friends!" Shaw pleaded. "Oh, I don't want to die, my friends! Let me go, and I'll leave the country forever! I promise to go to Mexico. Don't hang me!" He was pleading for his life, his lips moving rapidly. The color of his face was yellow-white.

"Don't call *us* your friends!" snarled one of the horsemen. "You woman killer! Mebbe *she* didn't want to die, neither. Throw that lariat over the big limb thar, Sid."

Shaw dropped to his knees, groveling in the sand. Two of the posse jerked him up by the shoulders. By this time, a hangman's noose had been made. It was cast over Shaw's head and tightened under one ear.

"The other one don't seem to be carryin' on much," the deputy sheriff observed. "He's just a kid, too."

"I'm not afraid to die," Sonny said softly, "but there's one thing I'd like to have you believe. I wasn't in with the King Johnny bunch. And I never saw this man"—he nodded toward Shaw—"until half an hour ago."

"You don't expect us to believe a whopper like that, do you?" the deputy demanded.

"It's the truth." Sonny shrugged. "I'm an outlaw, but I've never been guilty of cold killin'."

Crazy fear shone in Jed Shaw's eyes, but his heart was black and ugly to the last. "Don't believe him!" he gasped hoarsely. "The kid was in with us, all right. Why, he's the *hombre* that shot the woman!"

Sonny's eyes blazed, and he would have flung himself on the desperado, if the hands of both of them hadn't been tied.

"Got 'em arguin' among themselves," scoffed a member of the posse. "Come on, kid. 'Fess up, like your pard's doin'."

There was no trace of fear in Sonny's smile. "I've nothing to confess, *caballeros*. And if you're really goin' to hang us, I wish you'd get at it, or I'll have to insist on some breakfast first."

Shaw was lifted to the back of one of the posse's ponies. He would have fallen, if a man on each side hadn't held him in the saddle. The other end of the rope was over the limb and wound around the deputy's saddle horn.

"Let 'er go!" shouted someone.

"Don't do this!" screamed Shaw. "I don't want to . . . !"

The words died away to a gurgle, as the deputy spurred his pony, and the rope lifted Shaw from the saddle. In another moment, the killer's writhing body was thrashing wildly about in mid-air.

Sonny had witnessed hangings before, for in the hard outlaw life he lived such spectacles were by no means rare. This execution, however, made his heart beat fast. In a few moments, he, too, would be. . . .

Shaw's face was horrible, and Sonny turned his eyes away. All he heard was the jingling of the desperado's spurs. On the far riverbank, the early sun cast a shadow of the thing—a shadow that danced in a grotesque frenzy.

Four, five minutes passed. The body had ceased its struggles, but it spun rapidly around and around as the rope untwisted. The head was drooped down on the right shoulder.

At the end of six minutes, Shaw was cut down. He was

dead. The blackened face and staring eyes were covered with a bandanna.

"You're next, kid," said the deputy, turning grimly to Sonny Tabor.

Sonny had been straining at the rope that bound his wrists together behind his back. But it was useless. Death was waiting for him, and there was no eluding it. They lifted him to the fatal saddle, and the deputy adjusted the rope.

"You're game, all right," he admitted. "Anything to say before you swing?"

Sonny's heart was pounding, but outwardly he was smilingly cool and unworried. If he must die, he would meet the end bravely. He had lived as cleanly and honestly as the border country would let him, and he had no regrets.

"Nothing to say," he drawled. "And no hard feelin's. I reckon you think you're doin' your duty. Let's go!"

"Your name still Ex Wyzee?"

"It's still Ex Wyzee." Sonny smiled. He did not care to give the posse the satisfaction of knowing who they were lynching.

"Let 'er rip!" was the shout.

Sonny, when the tearful shock came, was hoping against hope that the jerk would break his neck. It hadn't broken Shaw's; the desperado had strangled in death horribly. And it didn't break Sonny's. He didn't lose consciousness when the terrific yank tore him free from the saddle. He felt his throat close as his head was forced over on the right side. Then came the terrible pangs of approaching death.

Sonny tried not to struggle. His open eyes could see the upturned faces of his executioners, the trees, the mountains, and the rising sun. It was his last look at life, he realized. All was over. Like a drowning man reviewing his past life, Sonny saw a thousand fleeting visions. Things were growing dark, and his throat and chest burned with searing pain. The sound of bells seemed to sing in his brain, tolling everlasting farewells—an everlasting *adiós* to life and youth. Then, as if from a great distance, he heard a shout.

"Cut him down, boys! Wait a minute!"

"All right, Sheriff, if you say so," the deputy grumbled.

In a moment, Sonny was on the ground. The noose was loosened, and he could breathe again.

II

Never had anything felt so good to Sonny as the cool mountain air. He drew it into his starved lungs in great, hungry gasps. His throat still ached, but he regained his self-possession rapidly. The posse was standing about him in a little ring, and there were seven men now, instead of six.

The seventh man, who had evidently just ridden up on a roan pony, wore a sheriff's shield on his leather vest. He was a man of fifty, hawk-eyed and stern of face. He was looking fixedly at Sonny and tugging thoughtfully at his gray mustache.

"You say he didn't make any statement?" he growled.

"The other one 'fessed up, but this kid was close-mouthed," the deputy spoke up.

"Did the other *hombre* tell you whar King Johnny and his men were holed up?" the sheriff demanded.

"No, but. . . ."

"A mighty smart posse!" cried the older officer with scornful sarcasm. "Why didn't you wait until I got here? We want King Johnny the wust of all."

"This kid, here, claimed he wasn't with the gang at the

Ferris murders," offered one of the men. "But we caught him with the other one, and we're sure. . . ."

"Oh, he's guilty, all right . . . guilty as blazes," snapped the sheriff. "And I approve of hangin' him. But I want King Johnny. This kid has got to tell us whar to find him." He examined Sonny Tabor's face with narrowing eyes. "I've seen this young *hombre* somewhar before, but I can't recollect whar."

"Wouldn't give his right name," said the deputy. "He's a game *muchacho*. You wouldn't think, judgin' from his baby face, that he was in on the Ferris deal."

The officer turned to Sonny. "I'm Sheriff Quinn," he barked. "I want you to tell what you know about King Johnny's hidin' place."

"I'm afraid I can't tell you much, Sheriff," gasped Sonny, who was still short of breath.

"You mean you won't."

"Suppose," Sonny demanded, "that I could . . . and did. Would that save me?"

Quinn rubbed his chin. "Well, I won't lie to you. You'd hang just the same. You got to pay fer your part in the Ferris deal. But if you talk, I'll take you back to Cactiville and jail you, until the court demands that I hang you."

"Heads I lose, and tails you win." Sonny smiled. "I guess I can't very well thank you for cuttin' me down just now, if I've got to go through all that again."

"If you don't talk, and talk straight," the sheriff thundered, "you'll hang right here and now."

Sonny's mind worked rapidly. He was in as tight a hole as ever, and yet while there was life. . . . The sheriff firmly believed that he knew something. Could he bluff the thing out? A plan was taking form in his mind—desperate and wild, but still a plan.

"You want to know where King Johnny's hidin', is that it?" he drawled.

"Exactly, and the quicker the better."

"Well," Sonny began, and purposely he talked rapidly, trying to make his words sound as confusing and vague as possible, "there's a range o' mountains west o' here, twenty-five miles across a mesa. I mean that you go up a cañon between two round-topped hills. . . ."

"What's that?" demanded Sheriff Quinn excitedly.

"Two round-topped hills, but first you got to follow a dry river up a cañon. You get to it just before you come to a place where two arroyos cut each other. There's a trail there, but it ends at the flat rock, as we'll call it. Six miles. . . ."

"Say, I can't make anything out o' that," the sheriff complained. "Can you, Frank?" he asked, turning to his deputy.

"He said twenty-five miles across to the mountains. He must mean the Green Tree range," said the other officer. "Then those round-topped hills. . . . No, I can't get it in my head."

"Tell us once more. Now go ahead with it," Quinn ordered.

Again Sonny gave them a jumble of hopelessly confusing instructions. He was, of course, only using an enormous bluff. He didn't know where King Johnny was, any more than the sheriff or his posse.

"If I could draw a map," said Sonny, when they had shaken their heads again, "I could show you somethin' that would interest you."

"Untie his hands Frank," said the sheriff after a moment's hesitation.

"But . . . ," began the deputy uneasily.

"Oh, it's all right. That's seven of us, and he ain't got a

gun, has he? I want to get this clear where the gang's hide-out is."

When Sonny's wrists were unbound, the young outlaw rubbed his numbed fingers until the blood began circulating again.

"All right." He smiled. "Thanks. Now I'll show you somethin' that might open your eyes wide."

He crouched on his haunches and, with his forefinger, began to trace something in the sand. The others watched, much interested.

"Here's the mountains I spoke of," he drawled, and made a figure much like the letter S.

"Uhn-huh," grunted Sheriff Quinn, nodding his head.

"Here's the lake, there," Sonny murmured, making a round O.

Sonny sketched something that looked like two Ns, then a roughly shaped Y.

"What's that?" puzzled the deputy.

"That's where the arroyos come in," Sonny explained, a twinkle in his eyes. "Here's the box cañon . . . savvy?" he went on, drawing a perfect letter T. "Now, Sheriff, I'm gettin' down to it. See this sharp-pointed hill?" Here Sonny made an A.

"The trail pass thetaway?" asked the sheriff, still suspecting nothing.

Before answering, the outlaw sketched something that looked like a B. "The trail makes a couple of curves here away from the cliff," he said softly, and then made another O. "Here's another lake an'. . . ."

"Lake!" snorted the sheriff. "Where d'you get that lake stuff? And two of 'em? I never heard o' no lakes around. . . ."

"Just a moment." Tabor chuckled, making the letter R in

96

the sand. "Does this map make sense now?"

Quinn stared at the inscription Sonny had traced. He opened his mouth to say something, but, instead, his jaw dropped. His eyes went wide. The others discovered what he did at the same instant.

"It's . . . Sonny Tabor!" they cried. "It spells. . . ."

"Hands up!" Sonny barked, his voice no longer easy and drawling.

Sheriff Quinn, taken off his guard for the moment, had made a desperate attempt to twist out of Sonny's reach. But too late.

Sonny had dodged him, snapped the officer's gun from its holster with his right hand, and thrown down on the six members of the posse. And at the same time, to prevent a deadly gunfight, if possible, he had passed his left arm across the front of Quinn's throat, pulling him in front of his own body for a shield. The sheriff, although struggling, was held helplessly.

"If there's any shootin'," said the young outlaw quietly, "lots of us will get hurt, includin' the sheriff here. Better put up your hands like good *hombres*."

Too astonished to resist, and realizing that the smiling gunman had the drop, the posse obeyed. The name Sonny Tabor had also thrilled them with fear. The fastest and deadliest gunfighter in the territory had them covered.

"*Bueno*," approved Sonny Tabor. "Now unbuckle your gun belts, one at a time. Throw away your Colts . . . throw 'em far!"

"I know now," groaned Sheriff Quinn, still helpless in Sonny's grasp, "why you looked familiar to me. I've seen plenty Reward posters describin' you. But you look so young, I just couldn't believe. . . ."

"Wish you'd let him hang, Sheriff," the deputy groaned.

"He's got us now. He'll shoot us down."

"Not at all." Sonny smiled. "All I want is my liberty. I don't know that it's ever tasted sweeter . . . thanks to your lynchin' rope. Just get tossin' your guns. You're next. Fine. Now I'll have to leave you." He released the sheriff.

He whistled, and in a second more he was on the back of his paint pony. He backed the animal to the spot where the deputy had tossed the guns, picked up one, and then shouted his farewell: "I'll square this, Sheriff, by catchin' the King Johnny gang for you, some of these days! I don't like 'em any better than you do!"

With that, he turned his pony swiftly and was off down the riverbed like a house afire.

"After him!" yelled the deputy furiously. "We mustn't let him get away! Why, he's made monkeys of us!"

"We was monkeys in the fust place," grunted Quinn in disgust. "Look at thet hoss o' his'n run. Catchin' that Tabor *hombre* ain't goin' to be so easy."

The posse did not catch Sonny Tabor. Sheriff Quinn's forecast proved to be correct. The posse lost no time in mounting and recovering their guns, but this took just enough time to give Sonny a start of a good quarter mile. After that, it was like hunting a needle in a haystack. Sonny's pony was much too fast, although the mounts of the pursuers were by no means slow. They had a few glimpses of him, once as he galloped over a rise, two miles away, and again at the mouth of a cañon, three miles away. That was the last they saw of him.

Sonny wasted no time in congratulating himself on his fortunate escape. He knew that an officer of Quinn's stripe would not give up after one day's failure. Sonny would probably meet that posse again. The youthful outlaw, however, was accustomed to being chased. Many a posse had burned the wind behind him to no avail. He left no more sign than an Apache.

When he was sure that he had shaken off the posse—for the time being, at least—he slowed his pace and headed eastward, making a wide circle to the north. He had enough provisions in his outfit to make sure of several meals, and he ate, shortly after noon, while Paint was drinking at Yavapai Spring—a tiny stream of cold water flowing on the eastern slope of the Azuls.

"I believe that was the narrowest squeak we ever had, Paint," he murmured as he mounted again. "That ought to teach us to be a lone wolf . . . always. If it hadn't been for Shaw. . . . Oh, well, he certainly paid for his crimes. Hangin's a terrible end, little hoss. Don't you ever do anything they can hang you for."

The little paint pony shook his head so vigorously the bit chains jingled.

At nightfall, Sonny made a careful camp, and before dawn he was on the trail again, headed deep into the mountainous regions of Arizona. He was not riding toward the Mexican border—the only spot where safety awaited him—but northward. Sonny loved his own country, in spite of the peril it held for him. He preferred it to the lazy security of Sonora. He had a particular destination in mind—the famous Turkey Track Ranch. Whenever he could, Sonny worked on the range. It wasn't long, as a rule, before the law ferreted him out and sent him on the dodge again. But Sonny never gave up hope of finding employment that would last more than a day or two.

The Turkey Track is in an out-of-the-way part o' the country, he mused as he rode along. *Maybe they won't recognize me there. I'll take a chance on gettin' a job, anyway.*

Toward noon, he found himself in a beautiful wilderness of luxuriant grass, towering cliffs, and broad mesas. Sonny had never visited the Turkey Track Ranch before, but he had a general idea where it was located. When he began to see cattle marked with that brand, he knew he was headed right.

Wonder where I'll find the headquarters of this outfit? he mused as he rode on. *They must have quite a bunch o' men on their payroll. This is one of the biggest ranches in Arizona, I reckon.*

He ate his midday meal on the banks of Poco Chico Creek, and, although the Spanish name meant "Pretty Little", it was one of the most cheerful streams Sonny had seen in all his wanderings. Clear cold water, and plenty of it, murmured over a gravel bottom.

After a ride of only fifteen minutes, he suddenly came upon an encampment of a dozen men. He was lucky in finding it at all—at least, he called himself lucky—for he had taken a rather roundabout route over a spur of mountains. There in a little hollow were the men and their ponies. He rode in boldly. Yet behind his easy carelessness was a brain alert for the smallest sign of danger. His probing blue eyes missed nothing.

"Howdy. This is a Turkey Track camp, isn't it?" he drawled.

Cowmen when on the job do not usually halt in the middle of the day to eat, and the fact that tin plates were being washed caused Sonny a little surprise. Still, every ranch has different rules.

Three of the dozen men in the little camp had sauntered forward to greet him. The rest watched curiously—a bit resentfully, Sonny thought. The right hands of the first three were near their guns. They eyed Sonny keenly before making any reply, then exchanged glances with one another.

"Yep," said one finally. "This is . . . er . . . cow camp Number Six o' the Turkey Track."

Sonny wondered at the faint grins that appeared on the faces of the other two at this remark. These men, all of them, were strange-looking cowboys. Their faces, for the most part, were hard and cold. They packed their guns low. Sonny sniffed. He smelled whiskey. Still, that was none of Sonny's business. If the owner of the ranch permitted it, it was his own right. There were many ways of running a big outfit like this one. No doubt cowpunchers of the better type weren't easy to get.

"I'm lookin' for a job." Sonny smiled.

"Oh, yeah?" The three looked Sonny up and down with narrowed eyes.

One of these men had but one eye; another had a broken and strangely twisted nose. The third member of this trio, however, attracted Sonny's attention most. He seemed to be the spokesman, the man in charge. He was not more than thirty, tall, with a well-knit figure. He was bareheaded, and his hair was black and wavy. A good-looking face was somewhat spoiled by a drawn-down, thin-lipped mouth. His eyes were like jet-black gimlets, penetrating and ice cold. Gun belts crisscrossed his waist. He was the only two-gun man in the crowd.

"I happen to be the foreman of the Turkey Track," this individual remarked, after a long silence. "What's your name, kid?"

Sonny gave part of it:

"Tabe . . . that's enough of a name, I reckon. Do I go to work?"

Several of the men laughed.

The man who had called himself the foreman studied Sonny for a moment, then nodded abruptly. "I think you'll do," he said meaningly.

Sonny dismounted to care for his pony. He had found a job, nobody had seemed to recognize him, and things looked bright. But in spite of all that he was uneasy.

III

"That's a nice saddle you got there, Tabe," observed the boss of the outfit, casting his eyes on Sonny's hull—truly a beautiful piece of workmanship, hand-carved and studded with medallions and silver butterflies.

"Thanks," said Sonny briefly. "When do I go to work?"

The same three men had taken Sonny a little apart from the others, who had remained lazily smoking and talking near the smoldering campfire. The raven-haired boss was looking at the man he had hired, and looking hard. He laughed at Sonny's question, and so did the other two. The one-eyed man's sides shook. The broken-nosed fellow almost spilled the tobacco from the cigarette he was rolling as he guffawed loudly.

"I don't quite savvy . . . ," Sonny began, his own eyes shining with dangerous little glints.

"I'm a pretty good judge o' men," interrupted the black-haired boss. "If I hadn't thought you was OK, well"—he shrugged expressively—"it would have gone hard with you."

Sonny wondered what he was driving at. He didn't have long to wait.

"You're a-runnin' from the law, ain't you, kid?" asked his questioner in a matter-of-fact voice.

Sonny's expression never changed, although he felt his heart leap and his pulses race. His voice, when he spoke, was even and cool: "And you don't want an *hombre* on your ranch that's runnin' from the law?"

Again the trio laughed. "Quit bluffin', Tabe . . . if that's your right name," the black-haired man leered. "I ain't got anything to do with the Turkey Track. None of us has. We're on the outs with John Law, same as you."

"Yes?" drawled Sonny, his mind busy. The warm glints in his eyes had not gone.

"You're welcome to join us," the leader of the outfit went on. "We lost a man yesterday, and we can shore use you, if you can shoot."

"And if I don't care what I shoot at," said Sonny grimly. "Would you mind tellin' me who you are? I'm plumb curious."

"I'm King Johnny." The raven-haired man grinned. "And this is my gang . . . the best set o' men. . . ."

"The best set o' killers and cut-throats in Arizona," finished Sonny, and he was not smiling now. "So you're King Johnny. Well, I happen to be Sonny Tabor, and here's where we mix."

At the name King Johnny went white. His eyes popped. But at the same time, he reached quickly for his guns, both hands darting downward for the notched handles.

"You want fight, do you, Tabor?" he snarled. "I've heard plenty of you, and here's where I. . . ."

It was the broken-nosed man who saved King Johnny's life, although it was at the expense of his own. King Johnny's draw had been lightning-quick, but compared with Sonny's the work of his hands was absurdly slow. Sonny's gun blazed viciously in two cracks of sharp thunder. The broken-nosed man, who had stepped between Tabor and

King Johnny, sagged forward in the burst of smoke, head rolling from side to side. He had been shot twice. Sonny was facing fatal odds, but somehow he didn't care. It was more than just recklessness. He was thinking of a woman fighting for her home—a woman ruthlessly shot down by these border killers.

The guns of King Johnny were out now. The one-eyed man was in the act of pulling a .45 from a shoulder holster. And the men at the fire, about thirty yards away, had scrambled to their feet, ready for battle. The first thought in Sonny's mind was to dodge to one side. For Paint, his pony, was directly behind him, and he didn't want the animal to get hit. Before he could move more than a step, though, half a dozen guns had blazed. Bullets whined about his ears. One grazed his thigh as he twisted his body about. Then a bullet struck him in the shoulder. Sonny sagged. It was a direct hit, and it was a wonder that he stood up at all under the sledge-hammer impact. His left-hand gun fell from his fingers, and he went back against his pony.

"Yah got 'im!" yelled one of the bandits.

Sonny fired once more. It was his last, but it was good. One of the desperadoes at the fire, in the act of raising a high-powered rifle to his shoulder, spun on his boot heels and dropped.

But that was the end. Sonny felt his knees fold up like oiled hinges. He fell backward, and only the paint pony kept him from sliding to the ground. The wound in his left shoulder was low and pretty bad. He saw nothing save gun flashes for a dark, agonizing moment—heard nothing but heavy revolver shots. His outstretched right hand, however, had closed over the saddle pommel. Paint, feeling the touch, started away at a hard run. The wrench nearly tore Sonny loose, but he hung on doggedly. Sonny never quite understood afterward how he got away. He did remember pulling himself up into the saddle; after that, most of it was a blank. All he knew was that Paint ran like a thing possessed. The wind sang in his ears, and he was weak and ill. That was all.

Hours must have passed before he came partially to himself again. There was no sign of pursuit, and the sun was low. The pony was swinging through a scrubby pine forest on a sloping hillside.

"We . . . got to get . . . somewhere, Paint," he muttered. "I'm afraid . . . I won't be able to stick on much longer."

He was losing strength fast. Where was Paint taking him? He had no idea where he was, or how far from civilization. He was not thinking, though, of himself. One thing bothered him. King Johnny and nine of his men were alive and free to carry on their careers of banditry and murder. He hadn't made good his promise to Sheriff Quinn.

The only schoolhouse in 100 square miles of Arizona wilderness nestled between two spurs of pine-clad mountains in the valley of the Poco Chico. It was a log building of one large room, furnished inside with a dozen small desks, two blackboards, and a few books. Building the little log schoolhouse had been the idea of John Williams, the owner of the Turkey Track, and his only daughter Molly was the schoolmarm. The children of the neighboring smaller ranches attended it.

It was Friday evening, nearly an hour after school. All the children had gone home, except one freckled boy of nine or ten, and he was there as a matter of discipline. He had to stay in.

"Cain't I go home now, ma'am?" he asked plaintively. "I'm sho' tiard o' sittin' heah."

"Don't say can't . . . say may I," reproved his teacher.

"Well, may I? Mah pop's got wo'k fo' me to do when I get home, sho' 'nuff."

"You should have thought of that," Miss Molly reminded him, "before you twisted the girl's ear, Little Texas."

"I don't like gals, anyway," muttered Little Texas, hunching himself down in his seat. "That's what ears are fo', anyways . . . to twist. Beats washin' 'em."

Molly Williams hid her smile and gave him a silencing look. She was pretty in a wild-rose way, and more than sixteen, and as fresh as any desert flower. She loved to teach school, even though it was hard sometimes. Pupils like Little Texas were hard to handle; their heads were full of mischief instead of knowledge. She was just about to send Little Texas home, when the clatter of hoofs broke the stillness of the forest outside. The door was open, and Little Texas craned his neck. A second later, he was on his feet.

"Miss Molly! It's a dead man . . . on a hoss!"

"Nonsense," she responded, but she hurriedly followed her pupil to the door.

The color left her cheeks at what she saw. A paint pony had halted so close to the schoolhouse she could have reached out and touched it. In the saddle, half in and half out, was a half-conscious youth, waxen-white under his tan, gripping the horn and bent over the pommel. His checked-blue shirt was spattered with red.

"He's been shot!" Little Texas cried. "He's sho' goin' to fall, if we don' do somethin'."

"Catch him. Take his other arm," gasped Molly, as the rider began to slip from his seat. She was a frontier girl, and her first fright was over. With the help of Little Texas, she managed to get Sonny Tabor—it was he—off the pony.

"Take him inside, won't we, Miss Molly?"

"Of course," said the girl in a matter-of-fact voice. "Who is he? Do you know?"

"Sho' a strangah to me, ma'am."

"We've got to help him!"

Sonny opened his eyes, half an hour later, with the feeling that he had come out of a weird dream. His wound no longer pained him, and, upon investigating it with his right hand, he found that it was bandaged. He couldn't place himself. Where was he? There was a roof over his head. That was queer. His first thought was that he was in the hands of the law and in jail. Then he saw the faces of the freckled boy and the older girl. He saw admiration in the first and sympathy in the other.

"You mustn't exert yourself," Molly warned him. "Just be quiet, and don't try to talk."

"But I feel a whole lot better." Sonny smiled. "Thanks to you. Did my pony bring me here? And, by the way, where is this?"

"The Forest Home Schoolhouse," Molly explained. "You've been shot."

Sonny smiled grimly. He knew. But the schoolhouse— that was a surprise. This girl who had cared for him, then, was the teacher.

"I live just a few miles from here, and my pony's outside," Molly explained. "I'm Molly Williams. My father, you know, owns the Turkey Track. I'll ride home as quickly as I can and bring help back."

This would never do. Sonny, above all, didn't want an investigation.

"I'd rather you wouldn't, miss," he said. "I'll go now. I

think I'll be all right. You see, I've been shot up some before."

"But. . . ."

"Miss Williams," pleaded Sonny earnestly, "I have just one thing to ask of you. You've done a whole lot for me already. But will you please say nothing about seeing me?"

"Why?" demanded the girl, meeting his eyes with her level brown ones.

"I have a reason, and I can't say more . . . now," Sonny replied.

"Well," she decided, "I will, if you will promise *me* something. You're not well enough to ride tonight. Will you stay here in the schoolhouse until tomorrow? I'll come back in the morning. It's Saturday, and there's no school. Your wound will open again if you try to go now."

Sonny thought for a moment, and then agreed. Molly had two more questions to ask: Who was he? And who had shot him?

To both of these queries, Sonny had the same reply: he could not tell her just now.

Before Molly and Little Texas left, they made him as comfortable as possible with blankets taken from his pony.

"Thanks, *muchacho*"—Sonny smiled at the freckle-faced youngster—"for what you've done for me, too. And you won't say anything about me, either?"

"I sho' won't, mister," Little Texas solemnly promised. Little Texas, feeling very much a man, rode part way home with his teacher.

"Say, Miss Molly," he cried, after a long silence, "I'll sho' bet you one thing!"

"What's that, Little Texas?"

"Bet you that *hombre*'s an outlaw."

"No," Molly said thoughtfully, "there's some mystery

about him, but I don't think he's done anything really wrong. Somehow he doesn't have a desperado's face."

"Cain't I come tomorrow, too, and see him?"

"Yes, but remember, not a word of this to anyone . . . not even your own father."

"Say," cried Little Texas indignantly, "what kind of an *hombre* do you think I am?"

IV

It was Saturday morning, and breakfast was being served in the big, roomy Turkey Track ranch house. As most of the ranch riders were away at their different cow camps, only four were at the table—John Williams, his wife, daughter, and the foreman, Dick Kane. John Williams was a big, hearty man of fifty, blessed with the vim and vigor of youth. Although his hair had turned gray, his clean-shaven face was unwrinkled, and his humorous eyes shone with energy. Molly looked much like her father, but she was small, like Mrs. Williams. The older woman was kindly and motherly. Just now, she was bustling between the kitchen and the dining room, carrying plates of eggs and bacon.

"You're shorely not goin' to the school this mornin', are you, Molly?" Williams asked. "Today's Saturday, isn't it?"

"Yes, Dad, but I have a lot of papers to go over today, and report cards to make out," Molly told him.

She had another reason, too, but she didn't tell her father of that.

"I'll tell one o' the boys to get your pony ready, Miss Molly," said the foreman quickly.

"You needn't bother. I think I'll walk today. It's such a fine morning."

The foreman shrugged. He was a gaunt, angular man of about forty. His hair was thin and sandy, and he wore a thick, blond mustache. Molly had never liked him; she didn't know exactly why. Her father, of course, trusted Dick Kane as he trusted no other man on the Turkey Track—and that was going some, for John Williams believed in the honesty of almost anyone. Dick Kane was too smooth and oily to suit Molly, who had a spirit and will of her own. Then, too, Kane was given to evil fits of cruelty. She had seen him beating a pony one day.

"I'm afraid you're working too hard at that school of yours, Molly," her mother put in. "You seem worried this morning, as if something was on your mind."

"Oh, I'm not worried," replied Molly hastily. She smiled. "And I don't know what I'd do with myself if it wasn't for the school. It's lots of fun, even if I do have to keep Little Texas Thompson in after school almost every day."

"That little rascal should be horsewhipped," said the foreman heavily. "He thinks he's smart."

"He's the teacher's pet"—Molly laughed—"but he doesn't know it. I like him. He isn't really bad."

Dick Kane wrinkled his nose in disgust and changed the subject. "Reckon they'll ever catch King Johnny and his gang?" he asked, turning to his employer.

"I hope so," replied Williams. "That Ferris outrage is one of the blackest crimes in the history o' the state. They killed a woman, I hear. Terrible."

"I hear that Sonny Tabor is somewhere around this district, too," Kane said. "He's worse than King Johnny, and then some."

"My land!" ejaculated Mrs. Williams. "I'm almost afraid to let you stay in that school all day the way you do, Molly.

110

With no men folk around, it's awful dangerous. . . ."

"Oh, I'll be all right, Mother." Molly smiled.

"Don't need to worry none, Maw," John Williams told them. "The Turkey Track's always a peaceful place, and I reckon it will stay that way. King Johnny's gang ain't within fifty miles o' here."

"But nobody knows," objected his wife.

John Williams grinned. "Don't be silly, Maw." He turned to his foreman. "What about this Tabor, Dick?" he asked. "What sort of outlaw is he?"

"Why, ain't you heard o' him?" demanded Kane. "He's a plumb bad *hombre*. Six thousand an' five hundred dollars in rewards for him, dead or alive. Most o' the sheriffs would rather see him dead."

"Is he really as bad as he's painted, though?" asked Williams. "I've heard a few stories. Just a kid, ain't he?"

"Just a kid, but he's murdered between twenty and thirty men . . . got Billy the Kid's record beat, I reckon."

"Maybe he had to kill in self-defense," Molly suggested.

"*Hm-m-m,*" sneered the Turkey Track foreman. "Don't you think it. He murdered and robbed an old man in Tucson two years ago. He's known to have shot a peace officer in the back . . . that was in Bowie. Not long ago, he killed a woman that befriended him, and. . . ."

"That's enough!" cried Molly. "I don't need to hear any more of his deeds. What a terrible man. I hope they do catch him, and hang him, too. I don't believe in hanging, but for such murderers as that. . . ."

"Hangin's too good for him," growled Kane.

Shortly after that, Molly left the table and got ready to go to her school.

As she walked along the narrow trail through the fragrant pines, she thought of what Dick Kane had said. What a cruel, heartless monster this outlaw killer must be. Sonny Tabor. She hoped that someday he would meet his just punishment.

Sonny greeted Molly with a smile. He felt better—almost his usual self, thanks to Molly's sensible first-aid treatment of the night before.

"Good morning," she said anxiously. "I was hoping . . . was wondering, I mean . . . if you'd be here. You're looking lots better."

"I think you saved my life, Miss Williams," said Sonny earnestly. "You and Paint together. If Paint hadn't brought me here. . . ."

"Who's Paint?"

"My pony." The young outlaw laughed. "I've been out to see him already this morning. He's hidden in that patch of cedars above the schoolhouse."

"Hidden?"

Sonny didn't like the way she repeated the word. What did she think of him, anyway? He awkwardly turned his hat about in his brown hands.

"Yes, miss," he said, two spots of color glowing in his cheeks. "I have to be careful. You see, I'm . . ."—he took the plunge—"I'm a hunted man."

"Oh," she gasped. "You mean . . . ?"

Sonny nodded. "I'm an outlaw," he admitted.

"I'm sure you . . . you've never done anything really wrong," the girl said after a long pause.

"I hope I'm not as bad as people think," replied the outlaw quietly. "I'd have to go some to be that bad. Honestly, though, I've never stolen . . . not a maverick or a penny. And I've never killed unless I had to do it." He paused, redder than ever. "I don't know why I'm tellin' you

112

all this, Miss Williams. It won't interest you."

"But it does," she said. "I'm very much interested."

"It's good to hear you say that. The fact is, I was forced into outlawry. And now . . ."—he laughed—"now the law won't let me be good. I wanted a job on your father's ranch, but. . . ."

"Why not?" She smiled. "Nobody needs to know who you are, and I'm certain. . . ."

"I think I ought to tell you who I am, though," Sonny said quickly. "I'm Sonny Tabor."

Molly started back as if she had been struck in the face. The silence that followed Sonny's confession lasted for almost a quarter of a minute. The Williams girl had whitened, and she edged away from the outlaw as if he were some unclean thing.

"You," she gasped. "You're . . . that killer?"

Sonny flinched. An ache greater than the throb of his wound tugged at his breast. This hurt. He was used to the hatred, the hostility of honest people. For years, he had known nothing else. But somehow this was worse than ever. Always he had tried to keep his name clean. Lies had blackened his name in spite of what he could do. He was a black sheep—an outlaw with a price on his head. And he would always be one.

"I'm sorry," he said in a low voice, "that you feel that way about me. I hoped you'd understand, and maybe be . . . a little different than the others."

"Oh, you don't need to be sorry!" Molly exclaimed in a scornful voice. "Besides, a man like you couldn't feel sorry. I'm not afraid of you, even if you are a murderer twenty times over."

"I'm shore you needn't be, Miss Williams. Would you mind telling me where you got the idea I was a murderer?"

Molly was almost in tears, but her eyes flashed now. "Why, everyone knows your record. I heard of it today. Mister Kane, our foreman, told us of some of your crimes . . . how you killed, robbed, and murdered . . . even the woman who befriended you."

"There's no truth in any of that," said Sonny quietly, although hot anger burned in his heart.

"I believe it's true!" cried Molly. "I hope they catch you! Go! Leave this place at once!"

Sonny put on his battered cream-colored Stetson, took one glance at the angry girl, and left the schoolhouse. Her words had stung. Never had he been cut deeper. He walked through the trees with his head down. The only friend he had in the world, it seemed, was Paint. Only the little pony understood him. He was bitter, and no wonder. What was the use of trying to go straight? Wouldn't it be just as well to live as other outlaws lived? He remembered the saying that you might as well have the game as the name. He was walking very slowly toward the spot where he had left his pony, when a voice hailed him. He turned and saw the freckled-faced boy running after him.

"Hello," said Sonny, hiding his troubles.

"Say, I just came from the schoolhouse," the little fellow panted. "Miss Molly, she done tol' me who yo'all was. She was mad, too. These gals ain't got nary bit of sense, have they, Mistah Tabah? My name's Little Texas. Shake!"

Somehow Sonny felt better. Gravely he shook hands with Little Texas.

"You're not against me, then, *muchacho?*" he asked.

"No, sah, I plumb admiah yo' a whole lot!" the freckled boy exclaimed in his Southern voice.

"Thanks." Sonny chuckled. "I reckon we men have got to stick together."

"Gals is loco," the youngster told him seriously. "The soonah yo'all fin' that out, the bettah. Say, Mistah Tabah, I got somethin' to tell yo'. Theah's a sheriff's posse ovah on the othah side o' the mountains. I 'spect they ah lookin' fo' yo'all."

Sonny's eyes gleamed with their old fire. He was himself again. The confidence Little Texas had in him—it was almost worship—made him see things in their real light. His jaw hardened. It wasn't too late to have it out with King Johnny yet.

"See heah what I brought yo'," said Little Texas, pulling a big Colt .45 from under his patched shirt. "I saw that one of yo' holstahs was empty, so I borrowed this from Pop, last night. Take it, Mistah Tabah, and show that ol' sheriff some smoke."

Sonny accepted the gift gratefully, but he was smiling thoughtfully when he spoke again: "Will you do somethin' for me, Little Tex?"

"Try me!" cried the freckled lad promptly.

"*Bueno, amigo mío.* Ride to the sheriff at once, and bring the posse here."

Little Texas stared as if he thought his ears had betrayed him.

"W-w-what? Yo'all ain't givin' yo'self up?"

"Not exactly." Sonny laughed. "Just leave it to me. You'll find out why later. Tell the posse I'm here. Tell 'em anything, but bring 'em here. You have a pony?"

Little Texas nodded, and with a last startled look at Sonny he turned and fled. Sonny knew that he would carry out the order.

Sonny Tabor had business on hand. He was riding Paint at a brisk pace down the valley, keeping out of sight among the timber. Although he did not remember much of his desperate ride of yesterday, he had some idea of where King Johnny's gang was located. He was sure that if he followed the lowland between the two ridges of hills, he would come upon the half-hidden spot where the killers were camped. There was, of course, a chance that the gang had moved, but it was hardly likely. Sonny was positive that he would find them at the scene of yesterday's battle.

Sonny's weakness had gone, and except for a numbness in his left shoulder and arm he felt as good as ever. And, thanks to Little Texas, he had two revolvers. He felt fit, ready for anything. Soon he began to recognize landmarks. He remembered the towering chimney of rock on the far side of the Poco Chico. The camp of the bandits must be close now. He turned off the trail, where the trees were even thicker, and presently he dismounted.

"Wait for my whistle, Paint," he murmured, rubbing the pony's nose. He stole down through the cedars on foot, slinking as stealthily and carefully as a prowling cougar. Yes, there was the camp. The gang was still there. He crept forward, inch by inch, until he could have tossed a stone among the men gathered there. A clump of thick brush offered him cover, and he took advantage of it, keeping low, until he could hear and see what was going on.

There was a stranger, a new fellow among the bandits. He was talking earnestly to King Johnny and the one-eyed man. He was a gaunt fellow, with a blond mustache and a slouch hat.

"We've been around here long enough, Kane," Sonny heard King Johnny growl. "It's time we was pullin' that job at the Turkey Track. You said you had things arranged for some easy *dinero*."

"I think I have," said the man called Kane.

"Well, bein' as you're foreman of the ranch, you ought

116

to know," complained King Johnny.

Sonny's heart skipped a beat. So this was the foreman of whom Molly had spoken—the man who had filled her ears with lies about him. Sonny wriggled a bit closer. What he heard interested him tremendously.

V

"Have you got anything special in mind, Kane?" demanded King Johnny, rolling a cigarette.

"I'm just tryin' to think," the Turkey Track traitor muttered. "If you'd be satisfied with what cattle I could. . . ."

"To hell with the cows!" said the one-eyed man.

"Exactly," snapped King Johnny crisply. "We want cash! We can't bother with cows now. The law's been hot after us since the Ferris deal."

"Say, by the way, where's Weld?" asked Kane.

"Shot. We buried him last night . . . Jonas, too. I forgot to tell you, Sonny Tabor was here. He got two of us in about two seconds."

Dick Kane's mouth opened in amazement. "Tabor, huh? He's bad medicine. Did you get him?"

"Yeah." King Johnny leered. "Ever hear of an *hombre* outshootin' me? I got him in the left side."

"Where's the body? There's above six thousand on him, stiff or breathin'," opined Kane.

"He managed to get on his pony, and we lost him in the woods," explained King Johnny. "Hunted most o' last night, but nary a trace. He's dead, though, now. I'd bank on it. He was bad hit. But let's forget Tabor for a while. What about the Williams deal? Do we raid tonight?"

"What's the good?" Dick Kane shrugged. "The Old Man

banks all his *dinero*. I expect he's got close to eighty thousand in the bank at Cactiville, but he doesn't keep much coin at the ranch. He's smart, old John is."

King Johnny and the one-eyed man swore disgustedly. The other bandits—eight of them—gathered around to listen. Sonny Tabor, too, was missing nothing of what was being said.

"I savvy ways to get money out o' men like him," snarled King Johnny. "The Apache Injuns taught me plenty tricks, I tell you."

"You can't torture the cash out o' the old fool, if he's got it banked," grumbled Dick Kane, rolling a cigarette.

"Say!" King Johnny's eyes narrowed to slits. "Has Williams got any children?"

Kane slapped his thigh and swore. "I never thought of that." He laughed hoarsely. "Have to hand it to you, King Johnny. Shore he has . . . a daughter named Molly. And the Old Man's crazy about her. If you could kidnap her, and hold her for ransom, you'd have things your own way."

"Can't we?" sneered King Johnny. "Why not?"

"It's dead easy!" cried Kane. "You can do it now. She's at the schoolhouse, four miles up the valley . . . alone."

"Then we'll pull the trick." King Johnny grinned. "Saddle up, all of you *hombres*. We'll hold that girl for a big price."

"I'll ride for the Turkey Track right now," said Kane hastily. "I want to be at headquarters when this happens, so Williams won't suspect. See you after you get the girl."

Kane quickly mounted and galloped away.

Sonny's hands gripped the handles of his Colt .45s. He faced a serious problem. His first thought was to open fire on the whole murderous gang. Never before had the thirst of battle burned so fiercely within him. But what if he were killed at their first volley? Who would protect Molly Williams in that case? No, he couldn't risk a fight now. Later. . . .

I've got to warn her, Sonny decided. *I've got to reach the schoolhouse before they do.*

He didn't dare attract attention by whistling for his pony. Already the gang was mounting their horses—a wiry, speedy remuda accustomed to burning up the trail. He didn't have any time to lose. Wriggling back into the trees, he ran toward the faithful Paint at top speed. He was panting when he threw himself into the saddle. The pony responded, and Sonny went tearing through the pines at a gallop. It was marvelous the way the animal twisted through the heavy timber. But no pace was fast enough for Sonny. He had farther to go than the bandits, but he soon circled around them and rapidly left them behind. And they hadn't seen him. They had no inkling that an outsider knew of their plans.

Paint was blowing hard when the schoolhouse was reached. Sonny dismounted at a bound and sprinted for the door. He didn't wait to open it. He hit it with his uninjured shoulder, and it flew open with a loud bang.

Molly Williams was at her desk, occupied with a stack of folded papers. At the young outlaw's impetuous entrance, she jumped to her feet with a startled cry. Then she recognized him. Sonny saw anger snap in her big brown eyes—saw her small hands clench.

"You back here?" she cried. "I don't ever want to see you again. I thought I told you that. Leave at once."

"Miss Williams," Sonny panted, "you must ride for home. Quick. There's no time to lose."

"Who are you to tell me what to do?" she asked scornfully.

"King Johnny and his bandits are comin' . . . to kidnap you!" Sonny gasped.

"I don't believe it."

"You'll have to, miss," Sonny pleaded. "You saved me, and now it's my turn to save you. They'll be here any minute!"

The girl was about to refuse again, but Sonny knew that there was no time for further talk. He took her by the wrist and, without heeding her protest, made her come outside with him.

"See that dust? Now do you believe me?"

She stared. Horsemen were galloping down the valley. A yellow, swirling cloud told of the beat of many drumming hoofs. Molly went a shade paler.

"But I left my pony home today," she gasped.

"Then ride Paint," said Sonny grimly. "He's the fastest thing on four legs. If you can ride. . . ."

"I can ride."

Sonny helped her into the saddle.

"But how about you?" she cried in alarm. "They'll . . . they'll kill you. I can't take your pony and leave you here."

"Don't worry about me, miss." Sonny smiled. "You ride that hoss."

"Promise me you'll hide from them," she pleaded.

"I'm not makin' any promises," said Sonny. "I'll try and keep them occupied and busy here at the schoolhouse. Ride."

"I'm sorry I misjudged you. I'm . . . I'm sorry I said what I did, Sonny Tabor."

"Never mind that." Sonny grinned, and he sent his paint pony away with a quick slap.

In a whirlwind of hoofs, Molly was headed up the trail toward the Turkey Track ranch house.

"Now," muttered Sonny, "it's me for it." He drew his guns and jumped for the schoolhouse door.

Sonny almost bumped into Little Texas.

"You back already?" Sonny cried, realizing that it was a poor time to have a youngster in the way. This was serious business—a fatal affair, more than likely. Why hadn't the little fellow kept in a place of safety?

"I'm sho' heah." Little Texas grinned proudly. "I sho' rode. Tol' the sheriff what yo'all said. He was sho' excited. Theyah headed this way, but I think theyah goin' to the Turkey Track instead of heah."

"I wish they were here," Sonny said grimly. "I'd give 'em somethin' to do. See those riders comin' up the valley?"

Little Texas shaded his eyes with a small tanned hand. "Sho' do. Who is it?"

"The King Johnny gang. Little Tex, hop on your pony and burn the wind out of here. Savvy?"

"Cain't do it, nohow." Little Texas grinned. "I saw yo' heah, and I sent mah pony home. I 'lowed I'd stick with yo'."

Well, it couldn't be helped now. Sonny chuckled inwardly, in spite of the peril that threatened. This *chico muchacho* was a lad after his own heart. He took Little Texas inside the schoolhouse and put him under the teacher's desk.

"Now, stay there, little *amigo*." Sonny laughed. "Don't move, and keep close to the floor."

"But I want to see the shootin', Mistah Tabah."

"There'll be plenty in a minute," Sonny promised.

Going to the door, he peered out. The riders were but a few hundred yards away now and out of the trees. Eight—nine—ten of them. They were all there. King Johnny was riding at their head.

Sonny saw that he was in for one of the fiercest gunfights he had ever had. The probable outcome—but he didn't stop to think of that. The time had come for action. The gang had drawn their ponies up outside, about fifty yards from the door, and was dismounting.

Sonny knew that the wisest thing he could do would be to start shooting at once, while he had the advantage of being under cover with his enemies in the open. He could not resist the temptation to meet King Johnny face to face, however, and to give him the most unpleasant kind of surprise. Some of them, at least, would pay for the Ferris outrage. It was men of King Johnny's evil caliber who made Sonny's existence so hard and full of danger and heartbreak. His own reputation suffered from their crimes.

The bandits were approaching the schoolhouse in a body, evidently believing that Molly Williams would be an easy victim. They had no inkling of Sonny's presence there. King Johnny was actually grinning.

The leader pushed the door open. The one-eyed man and another bandit shouldered through the opening with him; the others were just behind.

"Aren't you a little late for school?" Sonny drawled, stepping directly in front of them.

The bandit leader was astounded, the others no less so. King Johnny's eyes dilated, his face blanched. "Tabor," he gasped.

"Your teacher for today," said Sonny coolly. "Welcome to my gun school. I'm goin' to teach you a few things, and it won't be readin', writin' and 'rithmetic."

With an oath, King Johnny reached for his gun and his men did likewise. The odds were ten to one and they expected to make quick work of it.

It was then that the Forest Home Schoolhouse received

its baptism of fire. Sonny's blued .45s came sweeping up, spitting flame in a droning, sputtering roar. Lead began to fly. The terrific concussion of many guns shattered the windows at once. Smoke sifted down and hung in a dense, choking blanket close to the floor. Red streaks pierced it.

A rain of lead swept over Sonny's head, for he had dropped behind one of the desks. He was still shooting. He had a certain advantage, although a small one. The bandits were all milling about in the doorway, some trying to edge in, and others anxious to get out. Firing into the tangle, Sonny killed two of them.

"Drop him!" shouted King Johnny, white with rage.

Not too brave himself, the bandit leader had allowed his men to take the first furious burst of lead, dodging behind the one-eyed man. The words were hardly out of his mouth when another of the desperadoes went sagging down, reamed through the chest. It was becoming serious. It wasn't going to be as easy as King Johnny had expected.

The gang charged Sonny, but the jets of flame were coming from beneath another desk now. Sonny had rolled across the narrow side, jamming a handful of cartridges into the cylinder of the smoking gun as he made the dive.

The blackboards, chipped by half a dozen slugs, added to the din as they came crashing in pieces. A picture of George Washington, hanging in a frame above the teacher's desk, danced suddenly as the glass spattered in a tingling shower. A bullet hole had suddenly appeared between the eyes of the "Father of His Country", but Washington continued to look down on the mad scene with his usual philosophic calm.

A whiskery-faced bandit, shot through both legs, screamed horribly and blocked the aisle, his head banging the floor. Another of the evil horde stumbled over him, and

Sonny lined the sights as he went flopping down. Hot gun barrels. Sonny reloaded his second weapon as the gang hesitated. Sonny Tabor's six-shooters were taking a terrible toll. But King Johnny, desperate now and with the lust to kill glittering in his wicked eyes, urged them on. A bullet struck an inkwell over Sonny's head and sprinkled him with the blue liquid. A moment later, the one-eyed man spun around twice, his spurs raking the floor as he teetered back on his heels. A drool of red had appeared at his lips. He fell heavily, his head striking a desk.

"I'm gettin' you myself, Tabor!" grated King Johnny, jumping at Sonny through the smoke.

"Maybe," Sonny replied, and met him with flashing guns.

King Johnny, supposed to be one of the best shots in a showdown in all the state, had at last met his master. His Colts exploded, but the slugs screamed into the ceiling. For Sonny hadn't missed. King Johnny, shot twice in the left breast, stiffened out on the schoolroom floor. In the same second, Sonny had whirled his guns around to cover the remaining four.

"Put 'em up, unless you want more schoolin'!" he barked grimly.

The gang, with the leader dead and five others down, was whipped. One of the four survivors was wounded. All thrust their hands toward the ceiling under the threat of Sonny's twin gun muzzles.

"Reckon . . . we got enough," panted one.

They dropped their weapons. Sonny kept his Colts on them.

"Little Tex," he cried, without turning his head, "come and help me tie these badmen up!"

A freckled, grinning face suddenly popped out from behind

the teacher's desk. The eyes were shining. It was Little Texas. He stared about him. The schoolroom looked like a morgue. But if the sight bothered him, he showed no sign of it.

"That was sho' some gunfight, Mistah Tabah," he blurted, "and yo' sho' made a wreck of the schoolhouse."

"I'm sorry about that," Sonny replied sincerely.

"Well, I can't say as I am," Little Texas drawled. "It means that theah won't be no school heah fo' a week."

Excitement reigned at the Turkey Track Ranch headquarters. John Williams had tried to get in touch with his men, and failed. They were all out on the range. He had just mounted his horse and turned its head toward the Forest Home School, when a little cavalcade of horses suddenly appeared, filing down the narrow trail.

"Bring my Winchester, Molly!" cried Williams. "It's King Johnny's gang. Your friend Sonny Tabor is probably dead by now. They killed him, and are comin' here. No! Hold on, Molly! Wait!"

"It looks like most of them are tied to the saddles," breathed the girl.

"My land!" exclaimed her mother, who had run from the ranch house.

"Where's Dick Kane, anyway?" the old rancher complained. "I couldn't find him anywhere. In case of a fight, he could help us. . . ."

"There won't be a fight, Dad." Molly smiled. "Sonny Tabor and Little Texas Thompson are on that first pony. It looks as if they've captured those bandits."

Sonny reined up the pony he was riding and lifted his Stetson.

"Good mornin'," he drawled. "Hello, Miss Molly. Is the law here?"

The four captive bandits, bound securely to the saddles, were on four ponies. The body of King Johnny, limp and lifeless, was on another. Little Texas and Sonny were riding together.

The sheriff was not there yet.

"Shore you told 'em?" Sonny whispered to Little Texas.

"They'll be heah," said the boy. "I came by a sho't cut."

But by this time, John Williams had seized Sonny by the hand and was pouring out his thanks and congratulations.

"So you're Sonny Tabor, the *white* outlaw! My daughter told me how you saved her. I can't thank you enough. I can't begin to! Are you hurt, lad? Molly said there was nine or ten of them. Where are the rest?" he questioned.

"They're sufferin' from the same disease as King Johnny here," Sonny drawled. "A severe case of lead poison. Don't try and thank me, Mister Williams. I've done nothin'. Your daughter did more for me."

"I want you to forgive me, Sonny Tabor," Molly said, with tears in her eyes, "for all I said. I didn't know that. . . ."

"Just forget it, Miss Molly," replied Sonny gently. "We outlaws are used to bein' misunderstood. Little Tex, here, is the real hero. I couldn't have done much without that extra gun he brought me. By the way, Mister Williams, where's your foreman?"

"I was lookin' for him, too, just now," said Williams, puzzled. "Why?"

"He's in with this gang," said Sonny quietly.

The rancher was amazed. "You must be wrong!" he cried. "Why, Dick Kane couldn't have had nothin' to do with. . . ."

"Here he comes now," Molly whispered.

It was the foreman. He had trotted in on a black pony,

coming between the two corrals. He dismounted unsuspectingly, and strode toward them. Suddenly he stopped. They saw his face go white as wax.

"Hello," drawled Sonny pleasantly. He dismounted and sauntered toward Kane, who stood as if transfixed. "The little kidnappin' idea didn't pan out, you see."

"I . . . I don't know what you mean," faltered Kane, moistening his lips.

"Oh, yes, you do." Sonny smiled. "You are just as guilty as these others."

"Who . . . are you?" Kane gasped, his knees shaking.

"I'm Sonny Tabor," was the quiet reply.

It was a name to inspire terror, and the foreman seemed at the point of fainting. He got a grip on himself with difficulty and turned to his employer.

"Are you goin' to take this . . . this outlaw's word against mine, Williams? I swear I never. . . ."

"Aw, the jig's up, Kane," sneered one of the captive bandits. "We're all caught. Take your medicine."

Dick Kane, desperate now, suddenly reached for his gun. He was too slow. Sonny never even bothered to draw his own weapon. Instead, he lashed out with a solid left, catching the treacherous Turkey Track foreman on the joint of the jaw. Kane rolled over and over in the sand. Before he could regain his feet, Sonny, with Williams's help, had tied his arms with a lariat.

"I never dreamed . . . ," the old rancher began.

"Yo'all will find out a whole lot o' things," spoke up Little Texas delightedly, "with Sonny Tabor aroun'!"

At that moment, the drumming of galloping hoofs was heard from the other side of the ranch house. They had a glimpse of fast-riding horsemen, seven of them, through the cottonwood trees.

"It's the law, sho' 'nough!" was Little Texas's excited remark.

Sonny edged around to the corner of the house, alone.
He drew his six-guns, and, at the moment the riders flashed
around the building, he stepped out into the open.

"Hands up!" he snapped.

Sheriff Quinn—it was he and his posse—was taken by
surprise. But he and his men knew a dead drop when they
saw it. Their hands went up. The youthful outlaw's two
grim .45s were hint enough.

"Hands up again, you mean!" snorted the sheriff angrily.
"What was all this about, anyhow? A trap?"

"Not exactly. I hate to do this, *caballeros*." Sonny smiled.
"But I'm goin' to show you something that will make you
feel some better, anyway. Unbuckle your guns while I'm
explainin'."

The posse couldn't believe their eyes when they saw the
face of the dead man across one of the ponies. Sheriff
Quinn saw it first.

"It's King Johnny," he grunted, amazed and bewildered.

"You didn't get here in time for the fireworks"—Sonny
chuckled—"but I think I've made good my promise . . . to
bring this gang to justice. The prisoners are yours, Sheriff.
The others won't bother you any more."

"We . . . we were lookin' for you," gasped the sheriff.

"I know it," drawled Sonny Tabor. "That's why I'm
takin' your guns away. I figure you're got enough prisoners
for today without me."

Sheriff Quinn, in spite of his stern exterior, was a
sportsman. He laughed heartily. "When they told me how
slick you were, Tabor"—he chuckled—"I didn't believe it.
Reckon we know now. And we're plumb satisfied . . . and
more, too . . . to have the King Johnny gang rubbed out.

128

The Ferris murders are squared."

"And I reckon I'm squared with you, Sheriff," said the youthful outlaw, "for the near hangin' . . . my neck's still sore from the rope. Mister Williams, will you lead my paint pony over here? Thanks."

Sonny mounted, holstered one gun, gave his horse a pat, and headed it toward the south.

"*Adiós*, everybody!" he sang out. "Someday we'll meet again, *quién sabe?*"

Whirling about in his saddle, he waved his Stetson. There was a sudden cloud of dust as he swept around the bend and out of sight. He was gone.

Pride shone in Molly Williams's eyes as she watched him go. But Little Texas had something emphatic to say. He said it to the posse.

"If yo' law *hombres* want to learn somethin' about figthin', yo'all ought to go to school with Sonny Tabah fo' a while."

Sonny Tabor and the Border Blackbirds

A lot of water had traveled under Sonny's bridges by the time this story appeared in *Wild West Weekly* (6/25/38). He had traversed the Southwest several times over, been arrested and subsequently escaped from jail countless times, and managed to find the time to collaborate with several other *Wild West Weekly* characters, such as Pete Rice, Billy West and the Circle J as well as Powers's own characters of Kid Wolf and Johnny .45.

I

At the sound of the shots, Sonny Tabor reined in Paint and stopped to look and listen. Those heavy reports, roaring like low-pitched thunder, were as different from the high and ringing sound of rifle fire as day from night. No question about it, Colt .45s were doing the talking.

Sonny Tabor had thought himself to be alone in Devil's Basin. It was now nearly noon, and, since early morning, he had seen no living things except a few lizards, a couple of circling buzzards, and a rattlesnake. He was near the middle of a sun-baked sink in the extreme southwestern part of Arizona, below the Colorado. In Devil's Basin winter never came, and it was fierce summer nine months of the year. Now, although it was spring elsewhere, the burning sink was scorching hot and heat waves danced over the brown-yellow wastes. The ranges of barren, fantastically colored mountains seemed to flicker and waver uncertainly against the skyline. There was not a cloud in the bright and brassy sky overhead.

There were no more shots. It seemed to Sonny that they had come from the lava ridge, about a half mile away, toward which he had been heading. Paloverdes and desert willows were the only trees—if the meager and scrawny things could be so called—in all that vast expanse. They were a promising indication of water, and, as Sonny's canteen was empty, he had been looking for some such sign. But now he hesitated. Sonny had more reasons to be cautious than most men, for he was a fugitive from justice, wanted by the law. He would have to be careful.

"Let's take a look-see anyhow, Paint," the outlaw decided grimly. "Maybe it's just somebody with plenty of cartridges and a hankerin' for target practice. Anyway, we've got to find water."

There was no gunsmoke to be seen over the ridge, possibly because of the sun dazzle, but Sonny Tabor approached cautiously and used the mesquite and creosote bushes for cover. As he came nearer, he heard the hoarse and angry clamor of men's voices. He was climbing now among the trees, and the soft sand muffled the shod hoofs of his black-and-white pinto cayuse.

Paint knew better than to nicker at the scent of the water they were nearing. Like his master, the wiry little bronco sniffed danger, too. He remained quite still while Sonny dropped the reins and dismounted at the edge of the willow clump.

Giving a little hitch to his cartridge-weighted gun belts, the young outlaw stealthily wormed his way through the rank undergrowth that rimmed the spring-fed tank of water that glittered in the sun beneath him. As he did so, he nearly bumped into a tethered horse. The animal shied away from him with a snort, but there was so much noise from an open spot beyond the water hole that there was no danger of anyone hearing.

To Sonny Tabor's ears came bellowed oaths, the thudding of fists and boots on human flesh, and the choked-back gasps of a person being brutally beaten. A few yards farther, and the outlaw could see as well as hear. The first thing he noted was the body of a dead man sprawled out within ten feet of his place of concealment. He had just been shot evidently, for streaks and blots of crimson were still slowly widening over the front of his black sateen shirt. His upturned face was distorted by a cruel ugliness that even death could not dignify.

Sonny was more interested in the living. Beyond the pool, which was circular and rimmed with low grama grass, was an open space, and here a group of men were struggling. Or rather, four burly toughs were engaged in a mix-up with a lone victim. They had their man down and were pounding and trampling him unmercifully.

"Tamp 'im good!" snarled one of the mauling quartet. "We'll show him what happens tuh them thet kill a Blackbird! Bust in his ribs, Milt!"

Sonny Tabor's blue eyes, usually so mild and innocent-appearing, took on a cold and steely glint. The old bullet scar in his rounded cheek, the mark that so resembled a babyish dimple, puckered deeply as his lean jaw muscles tightened. The affair that he was witnessing was just a bit too one-sided to suit him. The man who was being manhandled was disarmed and helpless, but still conscious and trying to fight back. He was a lanky, sandy-haired man of about thirty, dressed in range clothes.

The others were decked out in a way that puzzled Sonny Tabor. All of them were wearing black shirts of either flannel or sateen, some of them double-breasted and ornamented by two rows of pearl buttons. Three of the men wore black horsehide chaps as well. One of them was a Mexican, and the others were riff-raff typical of the lawless border country, hard-faced and repulsive. All were armed with a least one six-gun.

The saddled horses of the party were scattered through the willow thicket and were cropping grass as though nothing were happening. They were desert-bred broncos like Paint, small and wiry.

Sonny made up his mind and came striding from the brush. He was wearing two Colt single-action .45s, and now he raked them smoothly from their low, thronged-down holsters. Their blued muzzles covered the desperadoes at the belt line, sweeping in slow and deadly arcs.

"Stop it," he ordered curtly. "I've got the drop on you. Don't make me prove it."

The four black shirts, hardly a dozen feet from him, whirled about in amazement. There was a burst of profanity, but there was no denying Sonny Tabor's unwavering .45s. One by one they lifted their hands.

"What the blazes?" one of them, a red-whiskered ruffian, gasped through bared teeth. "What . . . what you tryin' tuh pull, younker?"

Their bewilderment, for a moment, overcame their anger. Was it possible that this mild-looking young waddy dared to face the four of them? Sonny Tabor, in fact, didn't look dangerous—unless one happened to notice the deadly flame that burned behind his blue eyes. He was of slim, almost slight build, with the exception of a wide and powerful pair of shoulders, and looked even more boyish than his twenty-odd years warranted. He wore a checked blue-and-white shirt, brown *chaparejos,* and small Coffeeville boots.

Slanted over his left eye was the brim of his light-colored, ten-gallon Stetson.

"So you want to rescue this blasted Ranger, do you?" rasped another of the black band.

"Mebbe he's a lawman hisself," the red-bearded gunman suggested.

So it was an Arizona Ranger, an officer of the forces of law and order, that he was rescuing. Still, that would have made no difference to Sonny if he had known beforehand. He bore no grudge against the men who were sworn to get him, dead or alive. It wasn't a personal matter.

"All of you stand where you are," he told the black-shirted quartet.

The Ranger slowly got to his feet, staggering and blinking blindly at his rescuer. He was dust-covered, his clothing was torn, and his lean face was bruised and swollen.

"Thanks . . . thank you, kid," he blurted, trying to grin with his cut and mashed lips. "I'll take their shootin'-irons, while you. . . . Wait a minute!" he cried in quick alarm. "Thar's another! Look out behind you!"

Sonny went swaying forward at the impact of a bullet as the shot thundered out from the brush. A fiery twinge of pain went lancing through his left side and arm, and, as his knees buckled, he lost his grip on one of his Colts.

He spun about to face the direction from which the bullet had come, although he knew full well that the others would nail him when he did. There were five of the desperadoes, not four, and he'd been caught napping. Before he could send a shot at the man who'd surprised him, he was swarmed over by the others. Already reeling from the smash of the bullet, he was knocked flat by the onrush. Blows from fists and gun barrels sent blinding lights dancing before his eyes. The breath left his body as a boot landed in his ribs.

"Don't kill him, save him fer me!" rapped out the man who had fired the crucial shot.

He came toward the spot where the outlaw was being pinned down. While younger than any of the rest of them, this man was obviously the leader of them all. Sonny Tabor, who found it useless to struggle further, looked up at him dazedly.

"Jeff, this younker jist now tried tuh give the Ranger a help out," panted the red-bearded man. "He must be loco. Either thet, or. . . ."

"Lucky fer you Blackbirds thet I got here in time," said the leader jeeringly. "My bronc' tried to give me the slip an' I was out after him. Looks like this kid was doin' a good job of runnin' a sandy on you *tontos*."

The chief of the band had a black shirt like those of the others, and instead of *chaparajos* he wore chinks, a riding apron of buckskin decorated with silver embroidery. Two long-barreled Colts, one of which was still smoking, were held at his hips, close to his body.

"Who are you, half-pint?" he barked at Sonny Tabor, and then, as the outlaw did not reply, he dealt him a heavy kick. "Don't you know any better than to horn in on Jeff Morrell's Blackbirds?"

Jeff Morrell, as he had called himself, was a loose-lipped man of about twenty-three. He had hard gray eyes and a particularly vicious cast of countenance.

The Ranger had slumped back weakly to the sand. The bright hope that had been in his eyes just a minute before had given way to resigned despair.

"It's tough, kid," he told his fellow prisoner. "Thanks fer tryin', but it looks like you've got yourself in a mess on account of me. See here, you Blackbirds," he shouted at the desperadoes, "I don't care what you do to me, but let this fella go!"

"A pard of yours, is he?" leered Jeff Morrell.

"I never saw him before in my life," said the officer honestly.

"Well, you'll see plenty more o' him from now on," mocked the desperado leader. "Fact is, you're goin' to be right together when your time comes to die."

"What are you drivin' at, Jeff?" demanded a man the others called Roxbury. "Come on, an' let's finish the two of 'em! A couple of slugs through their blasted heads, an'. . . ."

"Would be too quick an' easy." Jeff Morrell laughed evilly. "I'm goin' to do it another way."

He bent first over Tabor, and then the Ranger, searching them for possible weapons. He appropriated the officer's wallet and money, and also relieved him of a pair of steel handcuffs. There was a jeering yell from the gang as Morrell dangled them.

"All right, Ranger, and you, too, button," Morrell taunted. "How do you like this?"

He snapped the cuffs around the Ranger's right and Sonny's left wrist, linking them together. The outlaw understood then what was in Morrell's mind. He meant to leave them there at the pool, manacled together, to face a lingering death by starvation.

"Catch up the bronc's an' let's git gone from here," Morrell ordered. "Git the Ranger's hoss, an' the kid's, too."

Paint had stood obediently when the reins had been dropped, and the loyal little cayuse was led from the brush. The red-whiskered man caught the Ranger's roan, and lead ropes were thrown on both animals.

"Give our regards tuh the buzzards," mocked the red-whiskered desperado.

"*¡Seguro!*" shouted the Mexican, a pockmarked ruffian named Bustamente. He was searching the body of the dead bandit, removing his guns and ammunition. "First the *muchacho* weel die from the hole in hees shoulder. Then the Ranger can drag him along weeth him wherever he goes. No?"

The others guffawed hoarsely. Leading the extra horses, they swung aboard and left the ridge at a gallop. They were headed south, and soon their dust was only a yellow haze on the far, heat-tormented horizon. Sonny Tabor and the man he'd tried to help were left alone and cuffed together at the water hole.

II

The outlaw's wound was very painful, but not serious. The bullet had very nearly passed between his arm and body without touching him. It had grooved his flesh a little, however, and his muscles were temporarily numbed.

"Well, son, what do you think of our chances?" asked the Ranger grimly. "Those devils took our guns, hosses, and they didn't forgit the key to these cuffs. I never thought they'd be used on myself. Lay your arm out straight, and I'll see if I can't bust the lock by poundin' it with a rock."

While the officer worked to break the handcuffs, Sonny Tabor considered the situation. It could hardly have been worse. Devil's Basin was in the very center of the dreaded Tule Desert, a good thirty miles south of the Gila River and the railroad, and it was very rarely visited. Even the Indians avoided that harsh wilderness. A walk of thirty or forty miles might save them, but how were they to make it? They had no means to carry water with them, and, even if they had, the prospect of such a journey was frightful to think about. By traveling at night they could avoid the worst of the heat, but their chances at best were slim.

What infuriated Sonny more than anything was the theft of Paint. He wanted to live now, if only to recover his pinto and punish the bandits who had taken him.

"My name's Ed Walton," said the Ranger. "What's yours?"

The outlaw didn't think it necessary to give more than an abbreviated form of it. "It's Tabe," he said. He spoke vaguely of being headed out Yuma way in search of work.

That was true enough, for Sonny wasn't a fugitive through any fault of his own. When he could, he worked at honest range jobs. He was going straight.

"I had a two-gallon water bag on my hoss, and a supply of grub," said Walton regretfully. "Well, it's no good to think of thet now. What are we goin' to do?"

"We can't stay here," Sonny muttered. "Maybe our best bet is to strike north toward the Gila. Those *bandidos* went south, though. I wonder where they're goin'."

"Thar's nothin' down thetaway but desert and jumbled-up lava." Walton groaned. "Way I figger, we're 'bout twenty-five miles from the line of old Mexico. Thet's prob'ly whar the Blackbirds are hittin' fer. Damn them ornery, low-down. . . ."

"How did you happen to mix with 'em?" Sonny asked, glancing toward the stiffening body of the sixth member of the somber-shirted desperado gang.

"I was lookin' fer 'em"—the Ranger shrugged—"but I didn't expect to come on 'em as sudden as I did. I got one of 'em, anyhow. Too bad it wasn't Jeff Morrell. He's wanted for three different murders, and it's hard to say how many more the Blackbirds, as they call themselves, have done. I reckon," he added gloomily, "that me and you will be included in the list. I can't bust this handcuff lock."

"Then we'd better not waste any more time on it," the outlaw advised. "We'd best start for somewhere. We'll never be stronger than we are right now."

"Whar to, Tabe?"

It didn't seem to make much difference. To the east were the far-off Mohawk Mountains, grim and forbidding, and on the west were the even more rugged, if nearer, barrier of the Tules. Finding help in that direction was out of the question, for across that range lay another desert, the baking Lechuguilla.

They decided to travel due south, following the trail left by the Blackbirds. It was a gamble, but it seemed as good a way as any, and Sonny was burning with anxiety to recover his pinto cayuse. Paint, to the outlaw, was something far more than just a horse.

They waited until the midday sun had become a little less intense, and then started upon their dangerous *jornada*, first drinking all they could of the unpleasantly hot and brackish water of the pool.

Cuffed together as they were, walking was difficult and painful. Before two hours had passed, both men were limping and footsore, and they were already thirsty. The steel manacle strained and pulled on their wrists, which had begun to swell and chafe. They had one thing to be thankful for, however. If Morrell had chained them left to left, or right to right, it would have made traveling even more awkward.

The sharp lava cut their boots, and the sand was blistering. Toward sundown, they rested for a while in the meager shade of a creosote bush, then pressed wearily on.

The tracks they were following still led straight to the south.

"How far do you think we've covered?" the Ranger gasped, as the great red sun was sinking at last behind the flaming Tules.

"Only five or six miles," said the outlaw cheerily, "but keep a stiff upper lip, *amigo*. There'll be a moon tonight, and it'll be cool. We can go twice as fast."

"I'm so hungry I'm as weak as a day-old dogie." Walton sighed.

"So am I," Sonny admitted. "Lucky they left us our matches. We'll eat."

"Eat what?" Walton snorted.

Sonny showed him. What he had to offer was far from tempting, even to starved stomachs, but it contained nourishment and would relieve their pangs for a while. The outlaw built a fire of mesquite and dead cholla joints and roasted a quantity of banana yucca, as Yaqui Indians often did when times were hard.

They pushed on again, feeling refreshed and encouraged. Before long the moon rose out of the southeast, flooding the immensity of the desert with soft, silvery light. It was so bright that they were able to follow the trail of the Blackbirds without much trouble. Hours wore by with heartbreaking slowness, and the moon grew small overhead. Not even the yammering of a coyote disturbed the brooding silence of the wastelands, and the only sound was the crunching of their boots. They seemed to be making no more progress than if they'd been walking on a treadmill. Always there were the same frowning mountains on their right and left.

"The Blackbirds seem to be headin' into old Mexico, all right," the Ranger panted. "Wonder what they'll be up to next. They say thet Tabor, the bad man, is in Mexico, too.

Leastways, we haven't had any reports on him fer some time now. Ever hear of Tabor?"

"Seems that I have," said the outlaw softly.

"He's a killer, they tell me," Walton went on. "I've never run acrost him myself. Well, it's them throat-cuttin' Blackbirds thet we're interested in now. It's gittin' light over in the east. Be daylight soon."

Sonny was sorry to see the return of the sun, for he knew the torture that it would bring. Their thirst was bad enough in the cool of the night, but presently it would increase tenfold.

At about ten in the morning they fell, exhausted and aching in every muscle, under a huge century plant for a rest and, if possible, a little sleep. Once again the Ranger tried to smash the handcuff lock, but he soon gave it up in disgust. It was already breathlessly hot, and in spite of their utter weariness they managed to doze.

Sonny awoke to find Ed Walton tugging at him. The Ranger's face, already bruised and battered from the beating of the day before, was enormously swollen, and his tongue seemed too large for his mouth.

"We . . . we'd better be movin' on, Tabe. We got to find water somewhars . . . or die. I cain't stand much more o' this. We should've stayed at the water hole."

The outlaw tottered to his feet. His lips were cracked and blistered and his throat was frightfully dry and painful. He managed to grin encouragement at Walton as they started out again.

Compared with their toil of the day before, their lightheaded progress was a nightmare. Everything seemed strange and unreal; the mountains seemed to sway and the flaming skyline to rock dizzily. Mirages filled the hollows with tantalizing visions of water. The Ranger began to talk out of his head at times. Once he fell, and it was all that Sonny could do to drag him to his feet and get him going forward again.

It must have been about three in the afternoon when Sonny's aching eyes focused upon a *bisnaga*. These barrel cacti were very rare in that extremely dry region, and this was the first one he had seen. Although the cactus was covered with rows of long and steely spines and he had no knife, the outlaw managed to smash in its top with a rock. Then, by churning the spongy interior with a mesquite pole, he collected a couple of pints of water. They drank that, and chewed the pulp.

"Maybe this will last us out, Tabe," muttered the Ranger, who was greatly helped by the pitiful little supply of moisture they had obtained. "It's lucky I'm cuffed to you . . . you'll pull me through yet."

There seemed to be some food value to the *bisnaga*, and they took all they could carry of the pulp as they started on again.

Sonny hadn't thought to look for the tracks they had been following, and he was surprised to see them still stretching out ahead of them. His flagging spirits rose a little. Paint had made some of those marks; he could recognize the prints of his small shoes, and, judging from the unevenness of the spoor, the pinto was acting up considerably.

The character of the wastes began to change, becoming less harsh and forbidding. The soap root and agave became larger and a few cedars appeared amid the twisted rocks. They were climbing now, ascending a broad valley where gnarled oaks and walnuts grew. They stumbled on, at each step finding the country more promising. At sundown they were in a brushy cow country, among foothills and arroyos.

"We're . . . clean out of thet gosh-awful sink," Ranger

Walton gasped. "We ought to come on somethin' soon."

And it wasn't long before they did sight something. Ahead of them, looming in the dim twilight, was the adobe headquarters of a *hacienda* There was a ranch yard, bordered by alligator juniper trees, and a couple of empty corrals. Sonny Tabor could almost smell fresh water.

They rushed forward, tripping over each other in their eagerness. If they had had the breath, and if their throats hadn't been so parched, they would have shouted with joy. Then their enthusiasm received a shocking setback. At the edge of the clearing, alongside the woven ocotillo fence, lay the sprawled form of a Mexican *peón*. His wide straw sombrero was crumpled under him and stained with scarlet. The man had been shot.

"Those Blackbirds, as they call themselves . . . they've been here ahead of us," blurted the horrified Ranger. "I'd almost forgot 'em. Mebbe they're still around here. Keerful, Tabe."

The sound of faint groans led them around to the front of the adobe. Entering through the smashed door, they peered into the darkness of the room. The Ranger gingerly scratched a match.

"*¡Hola!*" cried Sonny Tabor, who could speak Spanish like a native. "*¿Qué significa esto?*"

The flare of the light disclosed the figure of a well-dressed Mexican of middle age. He had been bound with lariat rope, one of his boots was off, and his foot showed signs of having been burned with a flat iron.

Sonny quickly learned all he needed to know. Jeff Morrell and his Blackbirds had raided the *rancho* and tortured the owner, *Don* Andres Lopez, into telling them the hiding place of his *pesos*. Then, with the money and all of Lopez's horses, the bandits had galloped away.

143

III

After the raiding of the Lopez *hacienda,* which was well over the line in old Mexico, the Blackbirds had cut back northward toward the International Boundary again. They had made camp at sunset in a grassy park high above the desert. With the exception of one member, the gang was in fine spirits. They had gained some 2,000 *pesos* and three good horses with very little trouble. The exception to the general joviality was Milt Chase, an iron-faced man with a knife-scarred cheek and broken nose. It was Chase who had taken it upon himself to subdue Paint and claim the pinto bronco as his own.

Several times that day Chase had straddled Sonny's horse, but he had never remained in the saddle for long. Paint had bucked and pitched like an unbroken mustang and had heaved Chase to the sand on three different occasions. Once the bronco had come very near biting the bandit's hand, and it was no wonder that Milt Chase, who imagined himself to be an expert with horses, was furious.

"I'll tame thet pinto, or kill him," he snarled, while some of the others were gathering wood for the supper fire. "Thar ain't no hoss ever made a fool o' me yit. I'll bust his spirit an' his head, too. Milt Chase will show 'im who's boss."

Jeff Morrell, looking up from cleaning his six-guns, grinned at him. "Funny thing about thet cayuse," he said. "He looks plumb gentle, but . . . look out."

Paint, in that respect, was exactly like his master. The pinto, along with the other horses, had been securely picketed in the grassy clearing. The rest of the animals were contentedly cropping the short, coarse grass, but not Paint. With indignant snorts he was waltzing around his picket pin.

The bandits called Roxbury and Towner were preparing supper and the others were talking over their next job, an important one, judging from the way they were discussing it.

"Two days from now." Bustamente grinned evilly. "That ees the time, eh? *'Sta bueno.* Thees time we make good stake."

"I wonder how the Ranger an' thet fool *muchacho* are makin' out long about now," sniggered the red-whiskered bandit. "Hurry with thet coffee, Rox. Say, Milt," he shouted to the frowning Chase, "you haven't unsaddled thet pinto yit! What's the matter? Are you afeared of 'im?"

With a curse, Milt Chase picked up a loaded quirt and left the campfire. His scarred face was distorted with furious resolve.

"Don't kill thet bronc', Milt!" Jeff Morrell shouted after him. "It's a right likely-lookin' cayuse, an' I'd like to have it myself after he gits used to us."

"I'm a-goin' to tame it, thet's all," Chase snarled.

But he approached Paint with extreme caution, just the same, for he dreaded the pinto's teeth, and he didn't like the look in the little horse's eyes.

"Now stand still, you blasted ringtail, or I'll make you fit fer a bone yard," Chase blustered.

He jumped forward, taking a savage cut at the pinto with his quirt, but Paint had dodged back out of reach. Again the bandit aimed a whistling stroke, and again Paint side-stepped craftily. Milt Chase's fury was rising by leaps and bounds.

"You've been a one-man hoss so far, *caballo,* but now you're goin' to change! You'll eat out o' my hand afore I'm through!"

"Yeah?" jeered Jeff Morrell, who was watching things

from a safe distance. "Jist be shore he don't eat *off* your hand. Better give up tryin' to tame 'im, Milt. We can sell thet hoss in Yuma."

Whack! Chase finally landed with his quirt, and Paint's black-and-white hide quivered at the slashing impact. That was the only sign of pain the animal displayed, however, and a change seemed to come over him. Paint no longer snorted or attempted to lunge away. The pinto moved closer to the picket pin in order to have plenty of slack in his rope and stood with his head lowered abjectly, as if willing to take well-deserved punishment for his misdeeds.

"I knowed I could break your spirit," Chase exulted, reversing his whip in order to deal the bronco a blow with the loaded end. "An' I'll bust it some more. I'll. . . ."

There was a terrific *thud*. Paint's hind hoofs, and not the quirt, had lashed out and landed. The wily little bronco had merely been tempting the desperado to come within range of his powerful heels. The force of the kick lifted Milt Chase three feet into the air and sent him rolling. There had been a snapping sound, like that of a breaking stick.

Before the swearing, screeching bandit could stagger to his feet, Paint had hit the rope, and hit it hard. Breaking free, the pinto went racing for the edge of the clearing.

Howling with pain and rage, Chase jerked his Colt six-gun from its holster. It spat flame and smoke, and a little handful of silky hair flew from Paint's flowing mane.

"If you're tryin' to crease him, thet was mighty close!" yelled Jeff Morrell. "Try ag'in, afore he gits clean away!"

"To blazes with creasin' 'im, I'm tryin' to kill 'im" yapped the desperado profanely. "Look!" he squalled, pointing at his dangling left arm. "The bronc' busted my elbow. I'll fill thet pinto's carcass with lead!"

His gun roared again and again, but Paint was going like

the wind, and none of the desperado's shots came close. In another moment the pinto, with an impudent flourish of his heels and a bugle of triumphant disdain, vanished into the scrub cedars. Paint had made a getaway.

IV

Morning found Sonny Tabor and the Arizona Ranger refreshed after a long sleep. After taking care of *Don* Andres, they had accepted his hospitality and had eaten and drunk until they could hold no more. With a file, they had removed the handcuffs without difficulty. Now, after a hearty breakfast with the rapidly improving ranchman, they felt themselves again.

"Well, we made it." Walton grinned as they walked together in the ranch yard. "Thanks to you, Tabe, we pulled through. Do you know thet we're in old Mexico? Thet's goin' to make it tough, gettin' them Blackbirds. I haven't got papers to extradite 'em, and I'd have to work with the Mexican authorities."

"Unless they happen to go back across the line," Sonny drawled. "And by the way, Ed, bein' as we're in Mexico, and you haven't any jurisdiction, I'm goin' to tell you who I really am."

The Ranger stared at him blankly. "Well, whoever you are, you're my friend," he said impulsively.

"Maybe you won't want me for a friend," the outlaw said quietly, "when I tell you that my right name is Sonny Tabor."

Ed Walton blinked incredulously, and his breath, when it finally came, was drawn out in an amazed whistle. He took a step backward, looking Sonny slowly up and down, as if totally unable to link this blue-eyed, smiling youth with the outlaw who had made that name so notorious.

"Damn!" he ejaculated at last, and then he extended his big brown paw. "Well, Sonny, what I said still goes. Here's one law dawg thet you won't have to worry about."

The outlaw's eyes were confused as he gripped the Ranger's hand. He'd hardly expected that. Usually, when his real identity became known, men turned against him. Ranger or not, Ed Walton was still his *amigo*.

They made plans for the future. First of all, they would have to get guns and horses. Then they would track down the Blackbirds, all the way to Yucatán if necessary. Walton would arrest them and turn them over to the Mexican law, for the bandits' last murder had been committed south of the border.

"I won't leave this country until I've got Paint back," said the outlaw doggedly.

The Ranger nodded understandingly, lighting up one of *Don* Andres's strong black *cigarillos*. It was a beautiful morning, and in contrast to the desert to the north the air was cool. A Sonoran yellow warbling was perched on the ocotillo fence, singing gaily. "I want to recover *Don* Andres's *dinero*, too, if I can," the Ranger said. "And we . . . say . . . what's this? Why, I'll be. . . ."

"Paint!" Sonny cried in delighted amazement.

It was really his cayuse, dragging a frayed and broken rope. The pinto had back-trailed in search of his master. Just like a homing pigeon he had returned, and he came through the open gate with a joyous whinny. A moment later and Paint was snuggling the outlaw with an eager, velvety nose.

"You rascal," Sonny whispered. "So you broke loose from 'em, did you?"

It would have been hard to say which of them was the happier, the pinto or his master. The Ranger was highly pleased at his friend's good luck. Sonny had not only recovered his pony, but his saddle was on Paint's back as well.

Sonny was still stroking the pinto's glossy neck when the clattering of hoofs suddenly drew his attention to the gate of the ranch yard. There was a surprised whistle from Walton. A party of five riders, all of them Mexicans, had cantered in.

"Looks like *rurales* . . . the mounted *policia* thet they've got down here," he muttered. "Don't worry, Sonny. You're safe. They don't know you."

The *rurales* came in formation, like crack cavalry, and made a fine spectacle in their neat uniforms and huge, silver-trimmed sombreros. Whatever their other abilities, they were certainly fine riders. They drew up smartly where Sonny and Ed Walton were standing, near the door of the ranch house.

"*Buenas días, señores,*" their leader greeted. He was a big man with a heavy black mustache. "I am *Capitán* Morales. You are *Americanos,* no?"

"My name is Walton," said the officer quickly, "an Arizona Ranger," he added, turning back his buckskin vest and displaying his small silver badge. "And this is . . . er . . . *Señor* Tabe."

"*¿Como 'sta?*" The *rurale* captain leader bowed respectfully. "I have been ver' happy to have worked weeth the Rangairs before."

The captain's eyes, however, were not on Walton, but were fixed with a peculiar intentness on Sonny Tabor. Their expression gave the outlaw a start. He was uneasy. While he was not wanted by the Mexican authorities, he knew that they had been warned to be on the lookout for him.

149

"It's mighty lucky you came, *Capitán*," Walton blurted, and he went on to tell the *rurales* of the Blackbirds and their murderous raid on the López *rancho*.

As the Ranger spoke, the captain nodded. He and his men had dismounted, and Sonny felt more uncomfortable than ever. Captain Morales's steady glance seemed to be drilling him through and through.

"The . . . what you call them? . . . Blackbirds . . . yes, we weel be ver' glad to help you capture them, Rangair," Morales agreed. And then, before the outlaw could make a move, he whipped out a six-gun and brought it to bear on Sonny Tabor.

"Tabe is not your name, it is Tabor," snapped out the *rurale* captain. "Your picture I have many times seen on *Americano* Reward posters. I have orders to hold you for *los Estados Unidos*. Search the prisoner carefully, men," he told the *rurales* in rapid Spanish.

Ed Walton was astonished at Morales's shrewdness. The *rurale* captain, it seemed, knew more about some Arizona fugitives than he did himself. As the *policia* began searching Sonny, Walton gave a cry of protest.

"You're mistaken, Cap," he insisted.

Morales was coldly polite. "I am not mistake, Rangair," he said. "Thees is Tabor, wanted by the law in *Estados Unidos*. He is my prisoner."

Sweat stood out on Ed Walton's lean face. An idea struck him. If possible, he would bluff the thing out. He might be able to outwit these Mexicans and save Sonny after all.

"You speak English good, Cap," he said, "but can you read it?"

The *rurale* leader shook his head and admitted that his reading was limited to Spanish only.

"Then I'll read this to you," the Ranger growled, looking very fierce as he drew an impressive-looking printed slip from a pocket of his *chaparajos*. "Tabor has been pardoned, savvy? And this here docyment is the paper thet proves it. It goes like this," he said glibly. " 'Office of the gove'nor. To whom it may concern. I have this day, under my hand an' seal, granted full and unconditional pardon. . . .' "

"*Hola*. Wait one minute," interrupted the captain. "I have a man who reads *inglés* ver' good. Pablo! Read to me what it say on the Rangair's paper."

"I'm sunk," Walton whispered to Sonny, who was grinning in spite of his unpleasant predicament.

"Thanks for the pardon, anyhow," the outlaw whispered back.

Pablo, a tall, sad-looking *rurale,* took the paper from Walton's hand, peered at it, and began reading in a loud voice:

Cattlemen attention! Big spring sale! Everything for the well-dressed gent! Try the Bisbee Mercantile's fine line of hats, boots, and long woolen underwear! Our prices are lowest. Our pants wear longest.

"Enough!" roared the *rurale* captain. "You try make fool of me, no? Rangair, I am much surprise," he chided. "If these is a sample of *Americano* jokes. . . ."

"Thet must be the wrong paper," said Walton sheepishly. "But listen now, Cap. I'm an American officer and Tabor's wanted by American law. You turn the prisoner over to me and I'll. . . ."

Morales shook his head emphatically. "My duty is to put heem into the jail at Tía María. Later, perhaps, when I have received orders, I weel turn him over to you, as you say. I weel send him now to the town weeth two of my men."

"But, you can't . . . ," Walton started to protest.

"Felipe, you and Pablo weel take charge of Tabor," said the captain authoritatively. "See that he is locked in the jail. Rangair, you weel come with me. We must try to catch those Blackbird *bandidos* you have told me of."

It couldn't be helped. Sonny was compelled to climb aboard his pinto bronco. Two of the *rurales* unsheathed their carbines and mounted their own horses at their chief's command.

"I'll come to Tía Maria and see you as soon as I can, Sonny," Walton muttered as he wrung the outlaw's hand. "I'll try and get around these Mexes somehow, and in the meantime . . . well, maybe I can find out somethin' about the Blackbirds. *Adiós,* pard."

Astride his newly recovered piebald bronco, Sonny Tabor rode away with the two *rurale* guards, bound for a Mexican jail.

V

It felt mighty good to Sonny, at that, to have his little *caballo* under him again. The outlaw was in good spirits, considering that he was headed for the discomforts of a below-the-line calaboose. It was good to be riding Paint, to feel the breeze in his face, and to hear the rhythmic drum of the pony's hoofs.

As he had been searched thoroughly for weapons, his two captors rode with their carbines in their saddle scabbards. They were armed with six-guns as well, however, and Sonny knew that they would be quick to shoot if he tried to escape.

Pablo and Felipe rode leisurely, smoking endless corn-shuck cigarettes. Sonny talked to them in their own language. Tía María, it seemed, was a small town about ten miles to the eastward. The jail there was very nice, the *rurales* politely told him.

"They will hang you when they get you across the line into Arizona, no?" Pablo yawned. "That will be too bad."

"It won't be so good," the outlaw agreed.

Unless he could get away from his *rurale* escort, or out of the Tía María jail, he would be sent across the border. The Arizona territorial court had already condemned him to death. It would be quite simple.

It seemed a toss-up, whether to die by *rurale* gunfire or wait for the hangman's noose. Ed Walton, of course, might be able to help him later, but, if he did, it would be at the price of his job, his honor, and Sonny thought too much of the lanky Ranger to want that. The mockery of it was the luck of the evil Blackbird gang. They had been let off scotfree, thus far at least, and they would probably escape punishment. Sonny's jaw went hard at the thought of them.

After riding three or four miles across country, they reached a narrow, rutted trail that crept along the side of a brushy cañon. South of them towered range after range of blue mountains, until they became misty in the distance. It was a lonely land, and the only living thing to be seen was a swooping caracara, that weird mixture of hawk and buzzard so often seen in the remote Sierras.

A few miles more brought them out on a rocky table land where the sun blazed fiercely. The *rurales* took drinks of water from their canteens and invited their prisoner to share it. Then they loped on again.

Feeling hungry, Sonny reached into his saddle pocket for a piece of *carne seca*. The dried beef wasn't there. Instead, the outlaw's groping fingers came in contact with something that sent a thrill racing down his spine. It was a Colt six-gun, judging from the feel of it a short-barreled .38. One of the bandits, of course, had stuck it in there while Paint was in his possession. What a break it was for Sonny Tabor.

"What do you look for, *muchacho?*" Felipe demanded. He had seen his prisoner search into the pocket and now he guided his bronco in closer.

"Oh, just looking for some meat I thought I had," Sonny replied easily, knowing that the time wasn't yet ripe. He would have to wait until he caught his guards completely unaware.

"When we get to Tía María, we get you very fine meal of many beans," Felipe promised.

For another mile or so they jolted along. Felipe began to sing, and Pablo joined him in a mournful tenor. Sonny waited until they were touching the high notes, and then with a quick motion he jerked out the single-action .38.

"*¡Alto!*" he snapped out. "I've got the drop on you. Pull up, and don't try reachin' for your artillery!"

The wailing love song of the two Mexicans ended in gurgles. Their complexions were too swarthy for them to turn white, but they became several shades paler. They halted and raised their hands shakily.

"Do not shoot," Felipe gasped. "*Ay de mi,* we will do whatever you say, *señor.*"

"*Bueno.*" Sonny smiled, his bullet dimple deepening in his bronzed cheek. "Get off your hosses. Don't worry. I'm not goin' to do any shootin' if you do what I tell you."

He relieved the two astonished *rurales* of their gun belts and .45s, leaving the carbines in the saddle boots. Sonny knew what it meant to be put afoot—he'd just had an experience like that—and he didn't want to inflict any unnecessary suffering on Felipe and Pablo.

"I'm takin' your hosses," he told them as he gathered in the reins, "but you'll find 'em tied about a mile down the trail, savvy?"

The Mexicans nodded their heads vigorously. They were extremely glad that the amazing young *gringo* didn't take it into his head to do anything worse.

"*¡Adiós!*" Sonny sang out to them as he drummed away back trail. "And if you take my advice, *caballeros*, you won't try to follow me!"

VI

A few hours later, Sonny Tabor halted his piebald bronco in the shade of some oaks on a hillside a few miles from the Arizona-Sonora border. He had left the trail after abandoning the *rurales'* horses as he had promised. It was now about three in the afternoon, and the heat of the sun was tempered by drifting white clouds.

"Well, Paint," the outlaw told his pinto, "after what just happened, I don't reckon we'd better complain any more about our luck."

Sonny had no intentions of returning to the Andres Lopez *rancho*. He didn't want to run into the *rurale* captain if he could help it. The best thing, he thought, would be to get across the line again into his own country. He'd had enough of Mexico for a while, and, although Arizona was dangerous for him, the law there wasn't as hot on his heels as in Sonora.

While Paint nibbled the grass that grew around the base of the oak trees, Sonny rested in the shade for an hour or so, careful to keep an eye out for any possible pursuit. He didn't expect to be followed by Pablo and Felipe, however. Sonny was a pretty good judge of human nature. The two humiliated *rurales* wouldn't return to their *capitán* for a while, either, he guessed, but would jog on into the town for a few drinks of tequila. They would need it before daring to face their chief and admit the loss of their prisoner.

"We don't want to fall asleep here, *caballo*." The outlaw yawned as he mounted again. "Let's go some more."

He smiled to himself. It was queer, discovering the .38 like that, just when it was needed so badly. Unwittingly some bandit had done him a good turn. Sliding his hand into the saddle pocket again, he found something else that hadn't been there when he had last straddled the pinto in Devil's Basin. It was a folder, a Southern Pacific railroad timetable.

He nearly threw it away, but a thought came to him. What was that folder doing there? Possibly there was some meaning behind it. Such gangs as the Blackbirds ordinarily didn't travel by train, so what were they doing with the timetable?

He thumbed through the dog-eared pages of the booklet. There was a map, and then long lists of the different stations where trains stopped and the hour and minute of their arrival. Sonny found some of it hard to figure out, but presently he saw a column of names he was familiar with, the names of the little depots on the division east of Yuma—Stoval, Kim, Pembroke. Then he saw opposite the name of another station, Salt Hill, a penciled check mark. The No. 17 train was also marked, as was the time it reached Salt Hill from the east: 9:16 a.m. On the margin was scrawled a date: THURSDAY, JUNE 2.

"That's tomorrow mornin'," the outlaw mused. "What

156

do they intend? Catch a train?"

Ordinarily no trains stopped at Salt Hill. It suddenly occurred to Sonny Tabor what those notations meant. The Blackbirds weren't planning to catch a train, but were scheming to rob one! At least, that was the way it looked to Sonny. He had reason to be pretty familiar with the ways of outlaws.

It was a long way to the railroad, but Sonny made up his mind to ride there if he had to stay in the saddle all night. He could warn the agent at Salt Hill, at any rate. While he had nothing to lose or gain either way, Sonny was taking quite an interest in the doings of the Blackbirds, and, if possible, he would spoil their evil game. He urged Paint on at a good pace, for he was anxious to cross into Arizona and at the same time avoid the desolation of Devil's Basin by cutting around it. Toward evening he found himself at the International Boundary. A sagging barbed-wire fence, most of it flat on the ground and half covered with sand, marked it here.

"Say, it looks like the smoke of a fire. Hold up a minute, Paint, ol' boy," he muttered.

On the Mexican side, in a clump of trees near a small spring, a party of men was camped and was cooking supper. Thinking that it might be the Blackbirds, the outlaw approached warily, loosening his borrowed guns slightly in their holsters. Then he grinned.

It was the *rurales*, the captain and his two remaining men. With them was Ranger Ed Walton, and nearby were their picketed horses, browsing peacefully amid the tall grass. The odor of the simmering food made the outlaw's mouth water as he cautiously neared the camp. He could see Walton, leaning glumly against the bole of a walnut tree.

Prudence urged that Sonny vamoose from the vicinity *pronto*. The outlaw, however, didn't always do the expected. He wanted Ed Walton with him. The Ranger was certainly needed, if the Blackbirds had planned a train robbery. When Sonny had approached to within fifty yards of the fire without being seen, he suddenly urged Paint forward.

"Sit tight, you *hombres!*" he cried sharply, whipping out the guns he'd taken from his recent captors. "You're covered!"

The *rurale* captain leaped to his feet with a loud oath, but he made no move toward a pistol, nor did his men. Their hands went up like the hands of puppets yanked by invisible strings. The *rurales* had a wholesome respect for *Señor* Tabor and his two leveled six-guns. He had a real pardon now, a pardon in each hand.

"Get on your hoss, Ed." The outlaw smiled at the Ranger. "Come along with me. You're in the wrong country."

A grin spread the Ranger's homely face from ear to ear. "Son, I knowed them *rurales* couldn't hold you," he chortled, "but I didn't expect to see you *this* soon."

"Wait a minute," said the outlaw as Walton started for his bronco. He sniffed the appetizing air. "While you're at it, Ed, bring a can of that grub along. I'm shore the captain won't mind. And be shore to fill up your canteen."

While the *rurales* fumed and swore, Walton did as Sonny suggested. Fortified with food and water, he climbed aboard the horse that had been provided for him by Captain Morales. Then the outlaw and the Ranger, riding knee to knee, went galloping across the line into Arizona. A few half-hearted shots echoed out behind them, but the two riders only laughed. The Mexicans dared not follow them into the United States.

"How in thunder did you do it?" Walton asked, when he could control his mirth.

Sonny sampled some of the steaming meat and frijoles from the can the Ranger handed to him.

"Paint had a gun for me." He chuckled. And then he told Walton in detail of the day's happenings. When he explained the railroad timetable, the Ranger whistled in amazement.

"The *rurales* and me was on the Blackbird's trail fer a while," Walton said. "We found a place whar they'd camped and follered 'em north a ways. Then we lost their tracks. We was just figgerin' what to do when you came roarin' up."

"We won't need to bother about their tracks now, *amigo,*" said the outlaw grimly, "because we know right where they're goin' and what they intend to do."

"Sonny," asked the Ranger suddenly, "will you help me blow the tail feathers out of them Blackbirds?"

"Don't ask me such loco questions. Of course I will. We're on our way right now to Salt Hill station."

VII

Before nightfall they had covered many miles of brush country. When the stars came out, they rested for a while and gave their broncos a rub-down and a chance to get their wind. Then they pushed on northward under a swollen yellow moon. In order to reach the railroad they would have to ride at a good clip all night long. Sonny knew that Paint would make it, but he wasn't so sure of the Ranger's bronco.

"Wonder why they picked the Second o' June to pull the

job," Walton grunted. "Mebbe they've got an inside tip thet the train will be carryin' an extry large amount of cash to-morrow."

"That's probably the reason," the outlaw agreed.

Fortunately the night was cool and good for traveling. Mile after mile of wilderness slid by as they steadily pressed on through the ironwood, catclaw, and mesquite. At last the eastern sky began to grow pink with the approach of dawn, and the stars dimmed against their graying background.

The Blackbirds hadn't taken Walton's cheap watch, and Sonny and the Ranger consulted it carefully and often. Both agreed that, if they were to reach Salt Hill by sixteen minutes after nine, the time of the mail train's arrival, they would have to increase the pace.

Walton's bronco was gaunted and nearly exhausted. Paint's condition was a little better, but three hours of grinding, under the Arizona sun, were still ahead. Both horses were game and responded nobly. Luckily for them, both their riders were experts and knew how to save their strength as much as possible.

It was a quarter of nine when they came within sight of the glittering rails of the Southern Pacific, five minutes after nine when they galloped up to the yellow-painted little depot on the Salt Hill siding. The only other building there was a still smaller yellow-painted tool house. There was no sign of the bandit gang.

"Mebbe they postponed the hold-up," the Ranger panted, half relieved and half disappointed.

Sonny's hunch was otherwise. Although they had seen no suspicious tracks, he had a feeling that the Blackbird flock was lurking somewhere in the vicinity. After all, the actual hold-up needn't take place at the depot.

Jumping off their blowing, lathered broncos, they

sprinted across the cinders and into the station. Their jingling spurs and tall boot heels made plenty of noise, and the station agent must have thought a cyclone had struck the place. He was a little man who peered nearsightedly at them through steel-rimmed glasses. He seemed as dry and shriveled as a mummy. Living at that remote desert whistle post, no wonder.

"What in tarnation do you rannies want?" he demanded irritably.

"Is Number Seventeen on time?" Sonny asked quickly.

"She's ten minutes late. I jist got the message from the next station east," piped the agent, and then he frowned suspiciously. "What in Tophet do you want to know fer?" he demanded sharply. "She never stops here at Salt Hill."

"Ten minutes? Good! Thet gives us some extry time," said Walton, showing the depot agent his badge. "I'm a Ranger, feller," he explained. "Have you seen anybody around here this mornin'? Any suspicious characters? We're lookin' for train robbers."

"God Almighty," gulped the railroader, "why, yes, I did see some men on horseback early this mornin'." He went outside with them and pointed eastward up the track. "They went behind that hill yonder, I think. I don't see so very good. Do you think . . . ?"

But there wasn't time for any more talking. A quarter of a mile east of the depot the track curved around the base of a brush-covered hill, an ideal spot for a robbery, and no doubt it was the one selected by the Blackbirds for their foray. Minutes were flying, and there was none to lose. The Ranger had started toward the weary horses, but Sonny had another idea.

"Is there a hand car in the tool house?" he asked the nervous station agent. "Then give me the key to it," he requested when the railroader nodded. "Let's ride the hand car up to the curve," he suggested to the Ranger. "If the gang sees men on hosses a-comin', they'll know right away that something's wrong."

"Go ahead, Sonny," the officer approved.

Inside the tool house, some overalls and other odds and ends of clothing belonging to the section men were hanging from pegs. Sonny and the Ranger hurriedly slipped into a pair of denim jumpers to disguise themselves, throwing their hats aside. Then they set the hand car out on the main line.

"I dunno much about these contraptions," Walton muttered, as he took hold of one of the handles. "What do we do now to make the wheels go round?"

"Just pump . . . and pump like blazes!" The outlaw grinned as he sent his side of the bar downward with a lunge that set the wheels spinning. "Let's hurry. I think I just heard the train whistle beyond the hill."

Leaving the station agent blinking and open-mouthed in front of the depot, they went breezing up the track, working the handles like mad. Up and down, down and up they went like two jumping jacks, while the rails hummed under them. They were facing each other, and Sonny was on the rear so that he could look ahead. Already he saw a black mushroom of smoke beyond the curve.

"We look like section hands from the waist up, anyhow," Walton panted. "Cowhands from the waist down. How are we doin'?"

"We're nearly at the curve," Sonny said, shaking the perspiration from his face. "Don't you hear the train? Have your gun ready, *amigo*."

There was a series of inquiring toots from the locomotive whistle, then a grinding and hissing of steam and brakes.

The engineer had evidently sighted some obstruction on the tracks.

Then the hand car swept around the curve. Sonny and the Ranger could see the train, just then jerking to a stop about fifty feet from a big stack of railway ties that had been piled onto the tracks. Black-shirted men with guns in their hands were running from the brush alongside the right of way.

"It's Jeff Morrell and his Blackbirds, shore enough," the Ranger gasped. "Come on, and let's put some salt on their tails."

VIII

The Blackbirds had planned the robbery carefully, to the last detail, and each bandit knew the part he was to play in the hold-up. Roxbury and the red-whiskered desperado hurried to board the engine, for their job was to subdue the engineer and the fireman. Milt Chase and Bustamente dashed to the express car. Jeff Morrell took up a position alongside the train. His duties were to oversee his gang's operations and to keep the trainmen and passengers inside the coaches. Just to show that they meant business, the bandits had already fired a few shots into the air and at the windows of the cars.

Meanwhile, Sonny and Ed Walton had pumped their lumbering hand car up to the barrier. As they jumped to the ground about twenty yards in front of the locomotive, they were spied by the red-bearded bandit.

"Blast them spike drivers out o' there, Jeff!" he shouted to the Blackbird leader as he scrambled up into the engine cab.

"They're harmless," Morrell offered, thinking that Sonny Tabor and the Ranger were merely a couple of section hands. "Stay back, you, or we'll kill you!" he roared at them menacingly.

A shot rang out from the locomotive, and the fireman, who had tried to hit one of the desperadoes with his shovel, came tumbling lifelessly from the cab.

"Throw down your weapons!" shouted the Arizona Ranger at the top of his lungs. "You're all under arrest!"

For the first time the gang understood who the two newcomers really were. Morrell stiffened with blank amazement, and there were yells of surprise from the other four. Sonny and the Ranger were the last men they had expected to see. The gang believed them dying of privation in the middle of Devil's Basin, handcuffed together and helpless. And now here they were, with guns in their hands.

"Fer the love o' blazes burn 'em down, man!" Morrell bellowed as the realization dawned upon him.

The somber-shirted gunmen took their attention from the train and turned it to Walton and Sonny Tabor, for they knew that there could be no robbery until these two unexpected interlopers were out of the way. They still thought the pair would be easy to handle. They quickly found out differently.

Guns exploded like rockets, flashing flame and swirling smoke. Ed Walton, with the gun the *rurales* had lent him, was shooting fast, and so was Sonny. The outlaw, with his fire-spouting .45s held at the level of his hips, had dropped into a fighting crouch and had slithered to one side. He moved along the track with the deception and skilled footwork of a pugilist.

Roxbury and the red-whiskered bandit jumped out of the locomotive cab and Sonny nailed them with a scorching burst that curled them against the side of the coal car. Roxbury dropped with a brace of bullets in his body. The copper-bearded desperado squawked with agony, slumped to his knees, but continued to shoot. He had been shot in the chest.

Jeff Morrell and Bustamente were shooting as fast as they could trigger their Colts, and most of their shots were directed at Sonny, who was a bit in the lead. The outlaw, however, was craftier in gun play than any of them. No gunman in the Southwest could match him. He had learned in a hard and desperate school. Blue whistlers were droning everywhere like crazed hornets. They ricocheted against the sides of the engine and coaches, and kicked up great spurts of gravel and cinders alongside the track. Salt Hill had become a madhouse of shouts, screamed oaths, and thundering guns.

Ed Walton finished the red-whiskered killer with a quick shot and sent Bustamente staggering with a bullet through the leg. The Ranger teetered, then, himself. Jeff Morrell had fired at him, and the Ranger's shoulder was nicked.

So far, the battle had been fought entirely in the open, but now Jeff Morrell made a successful dash for a telegraph pole on the railroad right of way. Walton flattened himself to reload his steaming gun. Seeing him engaged in that, Bustamente and Milt Chase thought it a good time to rush him. It was a mortal error. Sonny Tabor was backing up his friend with deadly, quick-talking Colts.

Milt Chase carried his left arm in a sling—a memento from Paint—but his gun was spitting venomously in his right hand. It crashed once, and then again. The first bullet zipped over Walton's head, the second howled skyward, for Sonny had ruined his aim with two swift shots of his own. Chase lunged at the knees and slid forward on his face. The

Ranger snapped the loading gate of his .45 and thumbed the hammer as Bustamente limped toward him. The Mexican spun on the toes of his boots and sprawled sidewise.

Sonny was splintering the telegraph pole that Jeff Morrell was vainly trying to hide behind. Morrell, unfortunately for him, was broader than the timber, and the coolly smiling outlaw sent lead ripping through both his shoulders.

"Get up your hands!" Sonny advised him. "Your men are wiped out! And we've got you!"

Morrell profanely told the outlaw where he would see him first, and he came out from behind the pole and came a-shooting. Sonny and the Ranger both swept the Blackbird leader with gunfire. Jeff Morrell was through. Pierced by four or five .45-caliber slugs, he rolled over and lay still, as limp and shapeless as a broken sack of bran.

"Thet settles 'em," Walton quivered unsteadily. "Four and twenty blackbirds, and we baked 'em in a pie. Or was thar thet many of 'em? Four and twenty. . . ."

"Better sit down a minute, pard," Sonny urged. "You're light-headed. Let me fix that shoulder up for you."

Now that the fracas was over, the trainmen and passengers began swarming out of the train, an awestruck, excited group. While Sonny was stanching the Ranger's wound, the conductor, fat and red-faced, came puffing up.

"I thank you, men! I thank you in the name of the railroad company and the express company! We all thank you! Man alive, but was that a fight!"

"Was it?" drawled the Ranger in a bored tone.

"You're Rangers, aren't you?" the conductor babbled on. "I thought so!" he cried, glimpsing the badge on the under side of Walton's vest. "What you did was mighty, mighty brave. As for you, young man," he said, pawing Sonny's shoulder, "you're going to make the head of the

166

Arizona Rangers mighty proud."

"I dunno as to that," Sonny drawled. "You see, I'm Tabor, the outlaw. What're the chances of hoppin' a ride on your train to Salt Hill station?"

After the passenger train had finally pulled away from the little Salt Hill depot, Sonny and his Ranger friend watered their horses in the shade of the tool shed. Paint was weary, but more than willing to go again, and Sonny thought it was high time to be following the tumbleweeds. He chuckled a little as he eased the girths and shifted the saddle a bit.

"I reckon it's *adiós, amigo,*" he told Walton. "Paint and me are goin' to amble on from here . . . and I don't reckon I'd better tell you where we're amblin' to."

Walton squeezed the outlaw's hand. To hide his emotion, he blew his nose violently in his dusty red bandanna. "What I said still goes, Sonny," he muttered. "Here's one law dawg thet you'll never need to dodge. You'll get a pardon someday, mebbe."

"If I do, don't try to read it to the *rurales.*" Sonny laughed boyishly. "Good bye . . . pardner."

And out into the forlorn wilderness of Arizona, with a cheery song on his lips, rode the Southwest's most-wanted badman.

Kid Wolf Rounds Up Sonny Tabor

This was the first of several successful partnerships between Kid Wolf and Sonny Tabor, appearing in *Wild West Weekly* (9/7/35). Kid Wolf, whose initial appearance in the magazine was in the story "The Gunman from Monterey" in 1928, also ended up being one of the magazine's most durable heroes for the next fifteen years. Kid Wolf (who was called "Kid" by his friends and allies, and would allow his enemies to refer to him only as "Wolf") was an independently wealthy rancher from the Río Grande who preferred to wander the Southwest on his huge horse, Blizzard, in search of those who might be in peril. Kid Wolf and Sonny Tabor would pair again in "Kid Wolf Rides with Sonny Tabor" in *Wild West Weekly* (5/2/36) and "Kid Wolf and Sonny Tabor—Saddle Mates" in *Wild West Weekly* (2/4/39).

I

With the jingling of bit chains, the tired and lathered horses of Sheriff Dougle's posse came to a rearing, stamping halt in front of the moon-drenched headquarters of the Box Q Ranch. The men dismounted stiffly, beating thick white dust from shirts and *chaparajos,* for they had just crossed eighteen hot miles of Arizona desert. The sheriff had set a grueling pace for his party. They had galloped hard. But now that they had reached their destination, none of them seemed in any hurry to go in.

Gathering into a little knot under a rustling cottonwood, they began to talk in subdued voices. They already knew what they would find in the house. For the one who had brought them the news was with them, a slim-built little chap of about fourteen. He was the nephew and only near relative of Sam Caldwell, owner of the Box Q. Davy's sensitive face was strained and white now. But for a youngster of his years, he was showing real self-control.

While the posse was still hesitating outside and fussing with their wearied broncos, the door of the big adobe ranch house was opened, and a man with a lamp appeared in the opening.

"Is thet you, Sheriff?" he called out.

"Yeah. Anything new?" Dougle replied.

"Nope. We've jist been sittin' tight, a-waitin' until you came," said the Box Q waddy. "I'll bet you're all hongry, ain't you? I thought you'd be, and I had the Chinaman fix up some extry bait. Come on in."

"*Bueno*. I reckon we kin take time, Hogar," grunted the sheriff, recognizing the Box Q foreman. "But if thar's to be a manhunt, we'll need plenty fresh horses. Kin you fix us up?"

"I've already tended to thet. I 'lowed you'd need 'em, and I had the men cut out the best cayuses on the spread. The bronc's are ready and waitin' fer you, Sheriff."

The sheriff nodded, glad that Hoke Hogar had carried out these details. Personally he'd never liked Caldwell's foreman much, but the man seemed reliable and thorough. At a time like this, it was good to have someone dependable at the ranch, and Hogar apparently filled the bill.

With Dougle at their head, the posse of eight men came trooping across the long, covered porch and into the house. Big as it was, they seemed to fill the lamp-lit room to over-

flowing. Besides the sheriff, only two of the party were officers, both of them being Dougle's deputies.

The others had been hastily sworn in at Buckhorn—
cowmen, most of them, but there were citizens, too, of the
county-seat town, the most prominent of them being Adam
Claymore, the banker. They stood about awkwardly,
blinking in the lamp glare.

"Are all your Box Q men here?" the sheriff asked.

"Yes, sir, all present, Sheriff," said Hogar, nodding toward the three other men who made up the spread's string
of cowpunchers.

"Good! I'll want to hear your stories later," grunted
Dougle. "Whar's the body?"

"Through the door yonder, in the next room," the
foreman told him.

Davy Caldwell began, for the first time, to show signs of
breaking down. He swayed, and, if the sheriff hadn't caught
him, he would have slumped to the floor.

"Cinch yourself up tight, lad," said the officer kindly.
"You've been a humdinger about it so fer."

The kid straightened his frail shoulders and made an effort to steady himself. "I'll . . . I'll try." He nodded. "But
I'm an orphan . . . an orphan now, shore enough. Sam was
more like a dad to me than an uncle."

Adam Claymore stepped up and patted Davy on the
back. He was a tall man of about forty, gray at the temples,
and with a long, thin face and pointed features. Claymore
never forgot his dignity as Buckhorn's leading banker and
was the only man in the posse not wearing range clothes. In
his tailed black coat, dusty but presentable, and his boiled
shirt and string tie, he looked strangely out of place.

"Don't you worry," he told Davy reassuringly. "I've had
business dealin's with Sam fer a long time. He was a great

friend. I'm goin' to help you in every way I can."

Claymore's offer seemed well meant, but young Caldwell shrank away from his touch as the unbroken pony shrinks from the hand it fears will master it.

"Yes, Davy, we're all your friends," said the sheriff as he turned toward the closed door. "You fellows go ahead and eat," he told the posse. "I see everything's ready. I won't be long."

As Dougle disappeared into the room beyond, the men took places at the long table that had been prepared for them, some sitting, others standing. Steaming coffee and plenty of warmed-over food had been brought out from the kitchen, and the hungry men attacked it like a band of famished wolves.

The supper was served by Ling Foo, the Box Q cook. He was a strange Chinaman, this Ling Foo, and was probably of some mixed breed. He did not have the smiling blandness of most of his race. He never smiled, never laughed, and seldom spoke. Two wisps of black mustache, needle-thin, dangled from his upper lip, adding to his peculiar appearance, and there was something cold and evil about his almond eyes—eyes that never seemed to blink. He waited on the posse, filling coffee cups and ladling out food in contemptuous silence.

"Thet chink gives me the creeps," whispered one of the sheriff's men in Deputy Johnson's ear.

"He'd spook Old Nick himself," the deputy agreed, speaking in a low voice. "Old Sam shore had some queer *hombres* a-workin' fer him, and I ain't shore whether the chink is the queerest or not."

As the deputy had said, the men of the Box Q spread were a queer lot. Almost any type of man could have been found in the border country of Arizona, but from Hoke

Hogar down to Injun Frank, the wrangler, this outfit seemed a tough one. The four were heavily armed and looked as if they would be handier at gun work than at the ordinary toil of the range.

Hogar, the foreman, was a thick-set and powerful man with bowed legs, long arms, and a close-cropped, bullet-shaped head. His bulging, low brow and undershot jaw seemed hewn from stone. He wore a stag-handled six-gun on the left side of his body, well in front, butt pointing to the right, showing that he used a cross-body draw. Hogar, whose reputation wasn't of the best, was reputed to be deadly fast with that .41 caliber he carried. He had been mixed up in more than one shooting fracas, and had always come off best.

The other three men were of the same hard type. Denver Jack Close was about twenty-two, with a flair for high-priced riding togs. He wore gray chaps, boots inset with gray leather, and a double-breasted shirt of the same color, piped at the seams with crimson silk. Denver Jack was dark, slender, and would have been handsome if it had not been for a certain veiled insolence in his eyes and the half sneer that was always on his loose-lipped face. Fred Graffman was an untidy specimen with red-rimmed, whiskey-shot eyes, a shock of sandy hair, and unshaven chin. Injun Frank was part Apache, wooden-faced and unfriendly. He smoked one corn-husk cigarette after the other, Mexican fashion, and talked only in piggish grunts.

At about the time the hungry posse had finished wolfing down their supper, Sheriff Dougle came into the room again, quietly closing the door of the death chamber behind him. He took a seat at the table, but, instead of eating, he took a paper from his pocket, called for pen and ink, and began writing.

"Bein' coroner as well as sheriff of this county might be convenient," he growled as he finished, "but it shore makes an awful lot of extry work."

"You want us to make our statements now, Sheriff?" the foreman asked.

"Yeah. Davy explained jist about everything, and I've got a purty fair picture in my mind, but everything's got to be done in the reg'lar way. This will be a sort of informal inquest, but I want the whole truth, same as if you was in court. You first, Hogar. What happened this mornin'?"

"Well, it was about noon," said the foreman, with a brief glance toward the other men of the Box Q spread. "We'd jist come off the Greenwater range, me an' the rest of the boys, and, as we rode up, we saw a stranger here a-talkin' to the boss."

"Then what? Go ahead," prompted the sheriff.

"Seems that this jasper wanted a job. He was a younker of about twenty, mebbe a leetle younger or older. I heard Sam say thet he had enough riders jist at present and thet he couldn't hire him."

"Whar was this conversation takin' place?"

"Right near the back door. The stranger kid was on his hoss," explained the foreman. "Old Sam said thet he was mighty sorry thet he couldn't give him a job, and he walked alongside the younker's cayuse as he went away, talkin' to him friendly-like."

There was a dry sob from Davy Caldwell. "It was like Sam. He was big-hearted, trusted everybody," he said.

"When was the last time you saw your employer alive?" the sheriff asked Hogar.

"It was right then, while Sam and the stranger was goin' on together slow toward the corral. Me and the other boys went into the house to eat. We all waited a bit, and then,

173

when Sam didn't show up, why, we begin wonderin', and Denver Jack and me went down past the old barn and . . . well, I reckon you know what we found thar. Sam was stretched out on the ground dead, and the stranger kid was gone. Ain't it so, boys?"

The other Box Q waddies nodded vigorously.

"I've knowed Hogar fer quite some time, Sheriff, and I'm shore his word is to be depended on," put in Adam Claymore, smoothing the lapels of his black coat and puffing on his stump of black cigar.

"I'm takin' care of this inquest, Adam," said Dougle a bit impatiently. He turned to Davy Caldwell. "Where did you say you were, son, when this was takin' place?"

"I was in the kitchen, helpin' Ling Foo," said Davy. "He'd asked me to, special. I reckon it all happened about as Hogar said. I heard the feller askin' my uncle fer work, and I got a good look at him."

"Have any of you any idea which way the stranger went after the killin'?" Dougle questioned.

"We tracked him a way, but we wanted to git the news to you, Sheriff, afore we done any more," Hogar stated. "Seems he headed up toward Peepsight Pass."

"Peepsight Pass!" ejaculated one of the deputies. "If *thet's* the way he went, we've as good as got him. We kin divide ourselves into two bunches and corner him between two fires."

"Oh, we'll get him, all right." The sheriff shrugged, turning to the Box Q men again. "How come thet none of you heard any shots?" he demanded.

"We wouldn't have been likely to hear none," said Denver Jack, lacing a brown cigarette. "The wind was blowin' pretty hard about thet time, in a direction away from the corral."

"That's so," Davy admitted, "and the windmill was makin' quite a racket, too, I remember."

"*Hm-m-m*, it seems purty evident thet the stranger murdered Sam Caldwell, either because he refused the job or for robbery," said the sheriff. "Did your uncle have much money on him?" he asked Davy.

"Only a few dollars, and it wasn't touched," Davy said, his lip quivering. "Sam wouldn't have hurt a fly, Sheriff. It was a cold killin' . . . cold an' crazy. Sam didn't even have his gun on him."

"Bad business," growled Dougle, biting at the drooping end of his thick blond mustache. "Now fer a full description of the killer. You all claim you had a good look at him. What was he like?"

"Not a very big younker. He was blue-eyed, light-haired, and purty brown from the sun." Hogar considered thoughtfully. "He weighed on the light side of a hundred and fifty, I reckon. He packed two guns, and seemed to savvy plenty about the pinto bronc' he was forkin'."

"A pinto bronc'," repeated the sheriff slowly.

"He had a big dimple in one cheek," Denver Jack volunteered. "Jist a *muchacho*, he was, but I guess he was a bad 'un."

"I got a good look at him through the window," said Davy. "And, gee, the way I remember him, he didn't look like no killer. I thought. . . ."

Sheriff Dougle had jumped to his feet. He was an easygoing officer ordinarily, not easily shocked. But now his big square face had turned from red to purple, and his eyes seemed to catch fire.

"Everything's explained now!" he almost shouted. "I've got the answer!"

"What do you mean, chief?" demanded Deputy Johnson,

and then something of the truth began to dawn slowly over his leathery face. "You think . . . ?"

"The young *hombre* thet murdered Sam Caldwell," Dougle roared, "is Sonny Tabor!"

The name was startling. The whole company had heard much of Sonny Tabor, reputed to be the deadliest gunman in the Southwest. Who in Arizona hadn't heard of him?

"Well, I'll be . . . ," gasped Hogar. "Thet baby-faced kid shorely couldn't be. . . ."

"He is, I tell you!" the sheriff cried. "That dimple you saw is really a bullet scar. Tabor fools everybody. He don't look dangerous, no. But today's business shows you what he is. By jingoes, I. . . ."

"Tabor . . . so it was Tabor thet was here," repeated Hoke Hogar under his breath, and the Box Q riders exchanged glances that were full of genuine amazement. Even Injun Frank grunted and blinked his astonishment, and Ling Foo's Oriental calm, for once, was badly shaken.

For a few minutes, everyone talked at once. But the sheriff was quick to quiet the confusion.

"We'll git him, dead or alive," he snapped, "but we've got to keep cool and do some straight thinkin'."

"Ain't thar a chance thet you're mistaken, chief?" asked one of the deputies. "You know, the last report we had of Tabor, he was up in the Grand Cañon country. The sheriff at Prescott. . . ."

"I don't keer what the last report said!" thundered Dougle. "Tabor done this, and he's our man! Tabor stays in one place jist about long enough to git his guns warmed up, and then he moves on. He's fast. Look fer him one place, and he bobs up in another. But this time, we know almost fer certain whar to grab him."

"But. . . ."

"You all know the Peepsight Pass trails," the sheriff went on. "He cain't slip through. We'll split up into two parties and fork into Cedar Spring. We'll git him either thar or on the way thar. Now with fresh hosses. . . ."

The sheriff stopped short. A knock had sounded on the door, and the nerves of the posse were so wrought up that every man reached for his gun. Then they all grinned sheepishly.

"Come in," invited Dougle.

All eyes were turned in one direction as the knob turned. The door swung open, and a tall young man—a stranger to all of them—stood framed in the yellow lamplight. He seemed surprised, but not taken aback, at seeing such a large gathering in the ranch house. He bowed courteously, doffed his wide-brimmed sombrero, and, when he spoke, it was in a soft and deliberate Southern drawl.

"I beg yo'all's pahdon, gentlemen." He smiled with a flash of his even white teeth. "I hope I'm not intrudin'. I only wanted to inquiah the best way to Tucson, bein' a strangah to this paht of the country. Mah name is Kid Wolf, from Texas."

II

The crowd at the Box Q stared at the newcomer in a way that was hardly polite, but only natural. For Kid Wolf, as he'd called himself, would have attracted attention anywhere. He was dressed in fringed buckskins, brightened with color, and tall-heeled boots ornamented with a lone star worked in silver studs were on his feet. A big Colt Peacemaker was on each of the Texan's trim thighs—.45-caliber guns of the single-action Frontier pattern in

thonged-down holsters. Twin rows of cartridges glinted
brassily in two criss-crossed belts, the weight of them dragging the guns even lower. Kid Wolf, in fact, despite his
quiet courtesy, seemed to be a man who could take care of
himself in any company.

"Why, shore, I reckon we can put you right," said the
sheriff. "Come on in! Did you say your name is Wolf?"

"I allow mah friends to use the first name, sah," said Kid
pleasantly. "I see from yo' badge that you ah an officah."

"Yeah, I'm Dougle of Buckhorn." The sheriff nodded.
"Seems to me I've heard of you, Kid. Aren't you the friend
of the underdog, sort of a soldier of fortune . . . ?"

"A soldiah of *mis*fohtune," corrected the Texan. "I'm on
the side of those who ah weakah or mo' unfohtunate than I
am."

"Good. We need you here, Kid," said Dougle heartily.
"I want you to meet my men." He chuckled, introducing
each in turn. "You came jist at the right time, if you're really on the side of the law and justice."

"I'm on the side of justice, sah," said Kid, "and that usually means the law. In fact, sometimes I've had to be a soht
of law of mah own. I'm afraid yo' ovahestimate me, though,
but I thank yo' just the same fo' the compliment."

There were notable exceptions, but almost every one in
the room had warmed to Kid, and friendly grins replaced
the curious stares on most of the faces.

The sheriff hastened to explain matters. "I want you to
help us catch a badman, Kid," he said eagerly. "An
outlaw . . . a killer . . . the worst in Arizona."

Kid Wolf's eyes seemed to be counting the posse, and he
seemed rather amused. They all noted that they were gray
eyes with little tints of blue in them.

"Seems to me, sah, that yo' already have mo' men than

yo' need just to catch one outlaw," he drawled. "I appreciate the honah, but I must decline with thanks. I'm really not an officah, yo' know, and, when I hunt down a man, it's usually on mah own."

"But this case is different," the sheriff urged. "We need every man we can git, because it shore ain't no ordinary desperado thet we're after. It's Sonny Tabor."

The Texan thoughtfully built a cigarette and lighted it before speaking. "I think I've heahd thet name . . . saw it on some Rewahd postahs on mah way into Arizona," he said. "So he's called Sonny? He's young then, sah?"

"But he's killed a man or two fer every year of his life," snarled Sheriff Dougle. "Thar's a sixty-five-hundred-dollar reward standing out fer him, dead or alive, and, if you help us, you'll git a share, besides doin' the territory a big service."

The idea seemed distasteful to Kid, and he shook his head. "No doubt this Tabah deserves death, as yo' say," he drawled. "But if yo' think I'd be interested in that kind of money, yo' have mistaken yo' man. If yo' will kindly put me right as to the shohtest way to Tucson, sah. . . ."

Young Davy Caldwell interrupted by jumping forward impulsively and catching Kid Wolf by the arm.

"You say you're a soldier of misfortune, a friend of justice. Then prove it!" he cried shrilly. "Help us square things with that murderer, Kid!"

"This is the only relation of the murdered man," explained the sheriff as the Texan glanced toward him questioningly.

"Theah's been a murdah committed heah, then?" inquired Kid Wolf, and something like a gleam of interest, or some other emotion, came into his steady gray eyes.

"The worst kind of murder," confirmed Dougle. "I'll

give you the facts." And he went on to recount the Box Q
tragedy briefly but forcefully.

Kid listened to the story, and, while the sheriff talked,
his attention seemed to be only half on what was being said.
The other half was fixed on the men assembled in the big
room of the ranch house. He seemed to be studying every
face and what lay behind it. Ling Foo stirred uneasily when
the Texan looked at him, although there was nothing unfriendly in Kid Wolf's expression.

"Come this way, Kid," blurted Davy Caldwell, when the
sheriff had finished telling of the slaying. "I want you to see
what's left . . . of my uncle. I'm shore you'll help us when
you've seen him. I'm shore you will."

Kid Wolf nodded and allowed Davy to lead him into the
room beyond. A candle was burning there dimly, flickering
at the head of the bed on which a silent figure lay, covered
with a blanket. With a shaking hand, the nephew uncovered
it.

"Thar . . . thar's what Tabor done, Kid," he choked.

The sight was a pitiful one; even a man accustomed to
seeing death would have been shocked by it. Old Sam
Caldwell had been a kindly, harmless old man; his face, dis-
figured as it now was, was composed and peaceful, although
the white hair was matted with brownish clots. He had been
shot three times through the body, at fairly close range, and
then the killer had given him a bullet between the eyes, to
make sure of his death. The last shot had burned the sight-
less eyes and blackened the skin. It was not a pleasant thing
to see.

Kid Wolf quietly covered it again with the blanket, and
then put his strong brown hand on Davy's shoulder.

"Are yo' all right, *amigo?*" he asked gently. "Anything I
can do fo'. . . ."

"I've already told you what you kin do, Kid, if you want to help me," Davy faltered. "Do you think it's fair to let Sam's murderer go without bein' punished for this?"

"No, son, I don't think it is," said the Texan grimly.

"Then you promise to help catch him?" asked the youngster eagerly.

"Yes, I reckon yo' can tell the sheriff that I'll join his posse," Kid replied.

Davy gripped his hand. "You're really all they say you are . . . a friend of the underdog!" he cried. "I'll get a fresh horse fer you, Kid . . . the fastest one of the spread."

"The fastest one on the spread, Davy, may not be fresh, but I'm stickin' to him," Kid Wolf said with a slow smile. "He's waitin' fo' me outside, and his name's Blizzahd."

III

Without knowing what had awakened him, Sonny Tabor found himself wide awake. He was rolled up in only a thin blanket; the night air of the high mountain country was bitterly cold. But he was used to hardship, and he knew that the chill hadn't aroused him. It was something else.

Almost before he opened his eyes, his hands were gripping the butts of his .45 six-guns. Asleep or awake, his nerves were tautly strung, attuned to danger, and his movements were by instinct, automatic.

The moon had gone, but the stars were fading, and the eastern sky was beginning to be tinged with just the faintest suggestion of color. It wouldn't be long, he realized, until daylight.

He listened, lifting himself on one elbow, but heard nothing. The night was still, except for the faint whisper of the stunted pine trees that grew along the trail edge. Paint—the outlaw's black-and-white-spotted pony—was moving restlessly about somewhere near him.

"What is it, *caballo mío?*" the fugitive murmured.

The wiry little bronco snorted at the sound of his master's voice, then came out of the shadow and reached down his head to snuggle the outlaw with his velvety nose. There was something more than just affection in the caress. Knowing that Paint was trying to tell him something, Sonny Tabor began to buckle his gun belts around his slim waist.

"So we've got to *vamos,* have we?" the outlaw muttered. "I wonder what . . . ?"

He put his ear to the ground and lay quietly for a minute. Earth is a better conductor of sound than air, and, sure enough, he heard a faint, subdued thrumming like the far-off beating of a snare drum. *Thuddity-thud thuddity-thud*—there was something breath-taking in that drumming, for to a condemned fugitive it was the drum of death. He raised his hand, could hear nothing, but when he put his ear to the earth again, the sounds were already louder.

It could mean two things. Only two kinds of riders pound leather at night—men of the law, and men against the law. Possibly a desperate gang was climbing the Peepsight Trail toward him, but Sonny didn't think so. Anyway, he couldn't afford to take chances. Capture, for him, meant a hempen neckerchief. Swiftly and yet carefully he began to saddle his little cayuse.

"How did they get on my trail?" he said, half to himself and half to Paint. "I thought we had the officers still a-guessin'. I'm certain that the old *hombre* I hit fer a job back at that ranch yesterday didn't know who I was. But still. . . ."

He remembered the three or four men who had galloped

up to the house just as he was leaving it. Probably one of them had recognized him from his description and turned in the alarm. That was the only explanation that he could think of.

Everything on that ranch had certainly been quiet and peaceful enough when he'd left. The old ranchman had even walked along with him as far as the stables, in order to wish him luck and apologize again for not being able to employ him.

Sonny had been hunted relentlessly since his earliest teens, since he had first become an outlaw. Other crimes had been chalked against his name—crimes of which he was as innocent as the first. So being chased by John Law was nothing new to him. He was disappointed, though, for he thought he'd thrown the authorities off his track. He'd been very careful of late, and only dire necessity had led him to ask for a job at the Box Q. For Sonny was on the straight trail, law or no law, and, when he could, he worked.

He tried to size up the situation that was facing him now. There was only one thing he could do, unless he stood his ground, and that was out of the question. That was to ride on up the pass and down over the other side. There was no hiding place along the way, not even one that could be used in the dark. He'd been over the ground, a year or so before, and he remembered the way perfectly. The trail was narrow, sometimes hardly a yard wide, and dizzy cliffs were on one side. A steeply sloping cliff bordered the other side—a climb that a man or horse could make, but ended against the wall of the mountain.

"We've got to make tracks, Paint, and *pronto*," the outlaw said as he flung himself into the saddle and started the pinto forward.

If he could beat his pursuers to Cedar Spring, all would

be well. Several trails led from there, and he could even strike across open country. Unless—the unpleasant thought struck him with an impact that almost took away his breath—unless he'd been trapped. If more of the law was waiting ahead of him to cut him off. . . .

Besides, although Sonny had been forced to kill many times in his desperate career, the prospect of taking life— even in defense of his own—always gave him an empty feeling in the pit of his stomach. Although the law usually did its best to send him into eternity, the outlaw had never killed officers, for he realized that they were only doing their duty.

He could hear the beat of hoofs below him now, and without putting his ear against the ground, either. But Sonny's pulses pounded as he felt Paint's wiry muscles ripple under him. Even a rabbit pursued by the hounds can feel the thrill of the chase. Another grim game with death was beginning, but there would be glory in that game if it was won.

"Let's say *adiós* to those *hombres* in a nice way, Paint, ol' cayuse." Sonny laughed gaily. He was trying not to think of what might be waiting for him at Cedar Spring. It was a good half hour away.

Fire winked from the pinto's hoofs as steel hit the rock of the twisting, treacherous trail. As sure-footed as a deer, the animal raced up the uneven ground as if he had been on the flat, so close to the brink of the chasm that Sonny could have stepped out of his stirrup and dropped 1,000 feet. The wind began to sing by like violins.

"It's the law, all right," the outlaw said to himself.

The trail writhed along the mountain cliffs like a serpent, doubling back and zigzagging until even a goat would have been made dizzy in following it. Rounding a sharp curve,

Sonny looked back and saw at least a half dozen black dots crawling along the spiral mazes below him. At least, they seemed to be crawling. He knew that in reality they were horses and men hammering at full gallop.

Sonny knew that he hadn't a great deal to fear from them. He had a good two-mile lead, and he had faith enough in Paint to know that he could hold it. Unless more of the posse were waiting for him at the natural trap that was Cedar Spring, he had the race won.

Sonny Tabor certainly didn't look like a man who could be wanted from one end of Arizona to the other. In his checked blue flannel shirt, brown leather *chaparajos* much worn by hard use, and his battered cream-colored Stetson, he looked more like a harmless saddle tramp.

It was daylight now, and Sonny was nearly at the top of Peepsight Pass, 3,000 feet above the desert that unrolled like a painted, wrinkled canvas to the dim horizon. The angry red rim of the sun was already showing above the low line of jagged mountains in the east.

Paint's clinking hoofs pounded on and on, and then they were at the top of the pass, a barren notch between two frowning walls of red rock. Whirling through it, Sonny found himself shooting down on the other side. The trail was just as narrow and winding as it had been on the ascent, only now the cliff yawned on the other side, and the smaller cliffs were not so sheer as before. Only a quarter of a mile now to the spring. Beyond that landmark, there was a rough and broken country in which he might dodge his pursuers, or, at least, find cover.

The trail was very steep as it dipped down toward Cedar Spring. Once Paint slipped, squatted, but regained his footing and plunged onward. The outlaw could see the foamy green mass of foliage that marked his destination. All seemed quiet there. In another moment now he would be there—past it. . . . Then the outlaw's heart almost froze. A line of riders galloped out of cover.

The worst had happened. He was boxed in.

A bullet ripped the air close to the outlaw's head as he dropped low over his saddle pommel and sent Paint sprinting forward. No use to go back. His only chance was to break through somehow.

"If we've got . . . to die . . . let's do it here," he gasped.

Cedar Spring became a blaze of gunfire. Bullets droned viciously, hoofs clanked against stone. Gravel and sand spurted as the pinto darted toward the thinnest part of the death line like a black-and-white lightning streak. Cedar limbs swished. Paint's breath came in grunts that sounded like sobs. For a split second, everything hung in the balance.

Then Sonny flashed through the gap. Loud yells went up from the posse, more shots came, but he had run the gantlet. Open country was ahead now! One more race. . . .

"They'll never catch us now, Paint," Sonny panted. "We've won."

For a little while, it seemed so. But when the outlaw looked back again, he saw a lone rider hanging relentlessly to his trail—a man in buckskins on one of the biggest, whitest horses Sonny Tabor had ever seen.

IV

Kid Wolf had been one of the men detailed by Sheriff Dougle to cut off Sonny's escape at Cedar Spring. Among the others, there were two of the men from the Box Q— Hoke Hogar and Denver Jack. All the other Box Q riders except Ling Foo, the cook, were in on the manhunt, too, but were with Sheriff Dougle's party. Even young Davy was along.

If the men under Kid's command had obeyed orders, the outlaw wouldn't have escaped. But due to the panic of one or two of the posse, Sonny had managed to break through. Out of the thirty or forty shots aimed at him, not one had struck him. Kid Wolf himself had not fired. Killer or not, Sonny was outnumbered a dozen to one, and the Texan was too much of a sportsman not to give the outlaw an even break for his life.

It was a different matter now, however. Tabor was making a getaway, and must be caught. Kid sent his huge white horse thundering after him, the others following far behind.

"Let's get him, Blizzahd!" the Texan commanded.

Blizzard seemed almost twice again as big as the average cow pony; he would have made two of Paint, with some to spare. The big white bronco had never been beaten in a race across country, and Kid was so sure of overtaking Sonny that he felt almost sorry for him. Before long, though, he began to change his mind. Blizzard ran like a thing possessed, but still he did not gain on that bobbing, elusive pinto bronco ahead. The landscape whizzed by dizzily, and saddle leather fairly popped as the white horse skimmed over rocks, stumps, and gullies, but the pinto held its own.

On the straightaway, the outlaw wouldn't have had much of a chance, but he was letting Paint take advantage of every twist and turn. He was a master horseman, and years of dodging had made him as cunning as a fox. Kid's jaw began to tighten grimly.

He's a great ridah. I'll have to hand him that, he said to himself as Sonny maneuvered again and managed to gain another precious fifty yards.

Kid Wolf was wondering why the outlaw didn't turn in his saddle and open fire. From what he'd heard—and it had been plenty—Tabor was a crack shot, and the range now wasn't so difficult.

The Texan kept his own .45s in their holsters, warily watching the outlaw's every move. Somehow he'd begun to feel something very much like admiration for this notorious desperado.

Another mile, and Blizzard had gained a little. Then the pinto unleashed a few more tricks, turned the tables neatly, and pulled away again.

"Blizzahd, ah yo' goin' to let that little broomtail show yo' its heels all day?" Kid urged.

Blizzard was doing his best, but so was the pinto bronco, and for several minutes more Kid Wolf neither lost nor gained. The rest of the posse was out of sight. It was a strictly man-to-man race, a showdown between horse and horse. Fate, however, was against Sonny and the pinto. In the badlands Paint might have shaken Blizzard off, but on the level the pinto couldn't match the speed of the white horse's long and powerful legs. A little valley now showed up ahead. Its floor was as smooth as a table, and there wasn't even so much as a cedar for cover. The outlaw had no choice, for the cañon walls came down on either side, too steep to climb.

The spotty bronco gamely took the bit in its teeth and made the best of it. With small hoofs thrashing fiercely, it ran like an antelope, kicking up a long and swirling cloud of dust. Kid Wolf saw it and marveled. But Blizzard was in his own element now, and, if Paint could outrun him across broken ground, Blizzard could certainly reverse matters in a clear field. Yard by yard, the great white horse began to eat up distance. Only eighty yards now—sixty—fifty. . . .

Kid saw Sonny turn in his saddle, caught the brown blur of his face for a moment. Kid expected smoke then, but the outlaw didn't draw his weapons. He pounded on, bent low over his pommel

I won't shoot until he stahts it, the Texan decided. *Theah's a bettah way.*

With an expert hand, he shook out a loop in his riata, gauging the distance with a practiced eye. He was just starting his whirl for the throw, when Sonny suddenly swerved his pony a trifle.

There was a flash—an echoing report. Kid Wolf blinked in astonishment. A bullet had raked the knuckles of his roping hand. Sonny had drawn and fired that shot with such amazing speed that Kid hadn't seen the motion. But he held onto the rope and finished the throw, although he was so bewildered that he couldn't remember, afterward, just how he did it. Sonny had flattened himself along his bronco's neck, but the cast was perfect.

There was a sudden terrific jerk, Blizzard went back on his haunches, and Sonny Tabor and his saddle both went rolling into the dirt. The girths had broken. The outlaw had been caught around the shoulders.

"Lucky fo' me," Kid gasped as he leaped to the ground and ran forward.

The fall had stunned the outlaw. Sonny lay in a little huddled heap, clutching in one hand a Colt .45 that was still smoking a little. The pinto ran on for some distance, then halted uncertainly.

So this was Sonny Tabor. The Texan looked down curiously at the unconscious outlaw, wondering if, after all, a mistake hadn't been made. He didn't look bad, lying there.

There was a sort of boyish, wistful expression on his face, Kid thought.

"I'm glad I didn't shoot him," he muttered before he disarmed the outlaw and tied him lightly but securely with the lariat. "I reckon the law should pass on his crimes, though, and not me. He sho' deserves hangin' if he killed Sam Caldwell."

He had just finished tying the prisoner when he heard hoof beats. The posse was coming up, led by the portion that had been at Cedar Spring. Hoke Hogar, the Box Q foreman, roweling a lathered horse, was some distance in advance of the others.

"Is he dead?" Hogar demanded jubilantly as he hammered up and swung out of his saddle.

"Just stunned, sah," said the Texan. "He. . . ."

Hogar jerked out his gun and fired at Sonny Tabor's head. Gravel flew up in a little red-tinged spurt and the outlaw drew up his knees and turned over on his side. Grinning, Hogar cocked his gun.

"Dead or alive, and it's better dead," he jeered. "I'll jist give him anoth. . . ."

Kid Wolf bounded forward and lashed out at the point of Hogar's unshaven chin. His hard fist landed with the speed of a whip crack, the power of a battering ram. With a prolonged grunt, the Box Q foreman turned up the soles of his boots, flopping over on his back, his gun landing a dozen feet from him.

"Yo' killah!" Kid's voice crackled.

V

Dazed for a few seconds, Hogar could only support himself, swaying drunkenly, on his hands and knees, his mouth dribbling crimson. Then he got to his feet, swearing venomously, and started to edge toward where his gun had fallen.

"Don't try that, sah. If yo' want yo' gun, pick it up and holstah it," the Texan warned. "I ought to make meat out of yo', and, if yo' make one bad move, I'll certainly do it, sah."

The rest of the posse had just come galloping up on their winded horses, and a crowd soon gathered about Hogar, Kid, and the motionless body of Sonny Tabor.

"What's all this? What's happenin'?" demanded Sheriff Dougle, breathing hard.

"I'd just taken Tabah alive, suh, when this sidewindah"—Kid Wolf jerked his head toward the sullen Hogar—"shot him. Anyone who'd kill a defenseless man. . . ."

"Aw, my gun fired accidental," growled Hogar with a poisonous glare at the Texan.

"Is Tabor dead, then?" the sheriff demanded.

"He's dying, I think," Kid said quietly. "I wish I hadn't taken any paht in this."

The rest of the party gathered closely about the fallen outlaw, awe and curiosity blended on their faces. Davy Coldwell, however, came up to Kid Wolf and extended his hand.

"I'm glad you did take part, Kid," he said. "My uncle's killer would have got away if it hadn't been fer you."

"Well, let's hope we've made no mistakes," Kid said softly.

A brief examination was made of the outlaw, and much to the Texan's relief the head wound Sonny had received from Hogar was found to be slight. The bullet had grazed his skull, cutting a groove that was hardly dangerous. The outlaw was completely unconscious, though, and would be for a long time to come.

There was a great deal of rejoicing among the posse over the capture. A couple of pint whiskey flasks were even passed around. But Kid Wolf took no part in the celebration. While the others talked and laughed, he occupied himself with catching up Sonny's game little cayuse and recovering the saddle.

"You done some mighty fine work, Kid!" the sheriff shouted at him. "I'll see thet you get a good big slice of the reward!"

"Count me out of it, if yo' please, sah," returned Kid.

"Don't let him fool you," sneered Hogar, speaking in a low voice. "He wants to grab it all. Thet's why he got sore when I fired at Tabor."

In spite of the sullenness with which Hogar, Denver Jack, Fred Graffman, and Injun Frank looked at Kid Wolf, the Texan was very popular that day, especially with the sheriff who couldn't praise Kid enough for his fine work.

Everyone accompanied the triumphant party into town, Sonny being placed, still senseless, on his own cayuse. It was only a little after noon when they drummed into Buckhorn, the county seat, a joyous, whooping band.

It wasn't a day that the little desert settlement was likely to forget soon. The news passed like wildfire that Sonny Tabor was in custody, and soon the dusty main street became jammed with excited citizens. Everyone craned his neck for a sight of the Southwest's "boy outlaw", and it was all that Sheriff Dougle could do to clear a way into the square stone building at the end of the street that served as a jail.

"Tabah is pretty sick, Sheriff," the Texan said. "Why put him in jail until he at least savvies what it's all about?"

"Kid, you mean well, but you don't onderstand Tabor like we do down here," snorted the sheriff. "He's slipperier than a side hill in a rainstorm, and I wouldn't have him git away from me fer ten thousand dollars. I'm goin' to hang him jist as soon as the death warrant is forwarded here from Phoenix, and, even if he's still senseless, I'll hang him. You can bet your boots I will."

Kid smiled grimly. He believed in justice, tempered with mercy. For some reason, the law down this way was mighty bitter, at least as far as Sonny Tabor was concerned.

The first thing the Texan did in Buckhorn was to turn Paint into the best livery barn in town and order for the courageous little cayuse the best of feed and attention. Kid had taken a great fancy to that fast-stepping half pint of a pinto.

"Jealous, Blizzahd?" He chuckled as he turned his own horse into an adjoining stall for a rub-down and a well-earned rest. "Well, yo' bettah be. You'd bettah be on yo' good behaviah, or I'll be makin' a trade."

Then the disturbing thought came to him that the spotty little bronco had lost his master forever, that Sonny Tabor would never hammer the mountain trails again.

Out on the street, he met the sheriff, surrounded by some of the posse. Their faces were flushed, and Kid quietly declined an invitation to join them in more drinks. Instead of going to a saloon, he crossed to a tiny restaurant and ordered something to eat. For some reason, he felt downcast, and, when he tried to whistle his favorite song— "The Río"—the tune, somehow, wouldn't come to his lips.

Although he hadn't eaten for twenty hours, he wasn't as hungry as he should have been. After he had finished, he sat staring thoughtfully out into the street.

He saw Hoke Hogar and the other three Box Q men in earnest conversation with a tall man in black clothes. He remembered the latter as having been with the sheriff's posse, too. It was Adam Claymore, the banker. It was queer about Hogar, Kid thought. Why had he been so cruelly anxious to kill Tabor? Kid carefully went back over the story of the Sam Caldwell slaying as he'd heard it. Could there be a false note somewhere? After all, only circumstantial evidence and the word of the Box Q hands connected Tabor with that crime, and the circumstances were pretty weak.

After a while, he saw the Box Q quartet mount their broncos and ride away in the direction of the ranch. A little later, Kid met Davy Caldwell, also getting ready to go home.

"Hadn't yo' bettah stay in town with me tonight, *amigo?*" the Texan asked the youngster.

"I reckon I'd better go . . . to my uncle. I think he'd want me to," said Davy gravely. "Thanks jist the same, Kid."

"I was wonderin' why you didn't ride with the othahs. They just left," said Kid.

"I'd ruther be alone. I don't like the bunch so well," Davy said as he swung aboard his pony. "Good bye. I'll be seein' you again soon."

Kid Wolf slowly rolled a brown cigarette and watched him jog away. For some reason, the Texan was feeling mighty uneasy. There was something wrong, and he couldn't figure out, just yet, what it was.

VI

A regular wagon road, fairly well traveled, led from Buckhorn to the Box Q and other ranches beyond. It was a lonely enough stretch of trail that dipped into a series of desert sinks and badlands. At about the halfway mark, however, it climbed upward through thickets of heavy brush. At this point, Hoke Hogar and his three pals, at a word from the former, called a halt.

"There's no use fer us all to be in on this." The foreman grinned.

"Well, how about us all gittin' in on thet red-eye, anyhow?" chortled Graffman.

A bottle was produced and passed around. It was a full quart, but a drink apiece finished it, and Hogar sent the empty bottle crashing into the mesquites.

"Is the road clear behind us?" he grunted.

"Yeah, he'll be along soon, though," said Denver Jack. "What do you say we draw straws fer this job? Matches will do," he said with an evil smile, taking a few from his pocket and breaking them off at various lengths. "Shortest match does the dirty work."

They drew lots, with Denver Jack himself getting the shortest straw.

"I'll bet you done thet apurpose, ol' hoss," guffawed the foreman.

"Shore I did, and why not? I don't mind doin' it," said Denver in a deadly cold voice. "Somebody's got to, ain't they? It ain't much of a chore. Fact is, I never did like thet leetle sneakin'. . . ."

"No gun play, mind," warned Hogar. "He don't carry no weapons, so it'll be easy to handle him. Come over here. I'll show you what."

He jerked his cayuse's head toward the left and led the way toward the edge of a steep embankment. A thin line of brush grew at the rim of a sixty-foot drop.

"Jist toss him over in thar," ordered the foreman. "It won't look like murder thetaway, see? Folks will think his hoss threw him. Another killin' on the Box Q would be too suspicious. This is the best place fer it."

"Adam Claymore says there'll be an extry thousand fer us if we do it," growled Graffman, his red-rimmed eyes glistening with greed. "Split four ways, thet'll mean. . . ."

"Five ways. You've forgot the chink. He's played straight cards with us so fur," said Hogar generously. "Say, didn't things turn out *bueno* fer us? I was afraid it would be purty thin, blamin' Sam's killin' on the younker that asked fer the job yesterday. Who'd have thought he'd turn out to be Tabor? Well, it cinches things fer us. The law's willin' to believe anything about him."

"Claymore told us not to do the job until we could blame it on somebody else," grunted Denver Jack. "I would have kilt Tabor in spite of thet Wolf jasper, Hogar, if I'd been you. With Tabor dead, we'd shore be safe."

At the mention of Kid Wolf, the Box Q foreman's ugly face became distorted with fury. "I ain't forget thet buckskin *hombre*'s buttin' in. I ain't forgot the haymaker he landed on me, neither," he snarled. "I'll git him fer it, jist wait and see. If the others hadn't rode up jist when they did, I'd have had it out with him."

Injun Frank had ridden back to the trail and was watching it with the stolidity of the Apache race to which he belonged. Now he rejoined the others, his face an expressionless coppery mask.

"Boy come-um soon," he announced. " 'Bout two miles away, come-um slow."

"We'll ride on, then," said Hogar, turning to Denver Jack. "You'll do what's got to be done, eh?"

"You don't think I'd slip up," sneered Denver, idly brushing a fleck of dust from his fancy shirt and carefully smoothing his gray *chaparajos*. "Say, why is Claymore so keen about gittin' the *muchacho* out of the way, too? I'd think old Sam would have been enough."

"Business reasons. With Sam dead, he could git control of the ranch ordinarily, see, but Davy's the heir, and the ranch would be tied up under a guardianship ontil he's twenty-one, unless Davy should die afore then," explained Hogar. "Savvy? I cain't say thet I do. But Claymore knows what he's doin', or he wouldn't be handin' us out no five thousand dollars."

"Adam Claymore's shore plenty smooth." Denver grinned, lighting a cigarette. "Well, *adiós*, boys. I'll be seein' you later. Tell Ling Foo to have a good supper a-waitin'."

When the other three had drummed on and out of sight, the self-appointed killer rode slowly down to the trail. Shading his eyes against the glare of the late-afternoon sun, he made out what the keen eyes of Injun Frank had noted several minutes before. Davy Caldwell, the fourteen-year-old nephew of the murdered ranch owner, was coming leisurely up the trail, unaware of the fate that awaited him.

Denver Frank waited smilingly for his victim. Murder to him was not a new thing. He enjoyed it, especially when he had every advantage his own way. He had the heart of a rattlesnake, and like a rattlesnake he enjoyed sounding a warning rattle before he struck. When Davy climbed the hill and rounded the turn, he came face to face with Denver.

"Why, hello, Denver," he blurted in surprise. "I thought you was with the others and home by this time." Fearful, he pulled his pony to a stop. Some nameless instinct had given him a warning.

"Yeah, I thought I'd stop and wait fer you, *muchacho*." Denver Jack's laugh was like the scratching of a file on rusty iron.

"Well, thet's nice of you, Denver," the youngster faltered.

"Yeah." Denver Jack smiled, his eyes as cold and dead as those of a fish. "I thought I'd wait fer you here, Davy . . . and kill you."

VII

Davy Caldwell's face went white, but, before he could whirl his horse, Denver Jack had reached out and seized his pony's bridle with his gloved hand.

"You . . . you must be jokin', Denver," the kid gasped, trying to smile at this joke. "You're allus sayin' funny things, Denver. You don't mean. . . ."

"Jist what I said, younker." The foppishly dressed Box Q rider leered. "Scramble down from your hoss!"

Instead, the terrified and defenseless kid jabbed his pony with his spurs. The bronco reared, but Denver had expected this move. He drove his own horse into Davy's mount and hooked a cruel right fist to Davy's head. The blow knocked him to the ground.

Denver dismounted leisurely, and, taking his helpless victim by the collar of his shirt, he yanked him to his feet and began dragging him toward the edge of the bluff.

"Over you go, Davy." He grinned. "If I had my way, I'd

have tended to this long ago. You was allus too cocky to suit me."

Crying out shrilly, the kid fought every inch of the way, digging his feet into the sand, beating at the powerful Denver with frail but desperate hands. He managed to hook his legs around a mesquite bush, but Denver only laughed and jerked him loose.

"I helped to kill Sam . . . and now I'm givin' you the same dose, banty!" said Denver Jack.

"Let me go!" screamed Davy. "Don't . . . !"

"Don't you like it?" the killer taunted as he took a fresh hold on the kid, in order to hurl him into empty space.

"No . . . and neithah do I, sah," crackled a voice from the trail. "Tuhn loose of him, yo' scoundrel. I'm givin' yo' a chance . . . to fill yo' hand."

"Wolf!" Denver croaked, releasing Davy and turning slowly.

Kid Wolf, mounted on Blizzard, was sitting motionlessly in his saddle, guns still holstered at his thighs. His gray-blue eyes seemed to shoot electric sparks. He was smiling, but with his lips only. There was no amusement in the icy stare that had fastened on Denver Jack.

"Draw, if yo' like, sah, but yo' had bettah draw . . . fast," Kid Wolf drawled.

Denver's face was as gray as his fancy shirt, and drops of sweat glistened on his forehead. A full half minute passed, with neither man making a move. Davy, scarcely breathing, had backed away. The very air seemed charged with storm.

Suddenly the storm broke. With his breath whistling through his clenched teeth, Denver Jack's right hand darted toward his holstered gun.

"If you're askin' fer it, Wolf. . . ."

His rasping voice was drowned out by the mighty

thunder of a Colt Peacemaker. Flame splattered from the level of the Texan's hip. He had drawn and fired before Denver's gun could leave its holster. With the roar of the shot, there came a dull, smashing sound as metal ripped through flesh.

The killer sagged to his knees, hugging his chest. Then, with a choked cry, he threw himself violently over on his back, splashing the sand about him with dull scarlet. Dying, Denver Jack rolled over twice in his last convulsion, and vanished. A moment later, Davy and Kid heard the *chug* of his body as it landed on the rocks at the bottom of the bluff.

Davy was unable to speak for a while. He could only look at the Texan and gasp. He was shaking like an aspen. It was the first time he'd seen death dealt to anyone, and on top of his own narrow escape it was a bit too much for his nerves.

"Buck up, *compadre*," drawled Kid as he slid the .45 back into its holster. "I had a hunch I'd bettah follow yo', and it's lucky that I did. Wheah ah the othahs? Were they in on this?"

As Davy was still unable to answer, Kid rode off to search the surrounding brush. He quickly returned.

"Feel bettah now?"

"You . . . you shore saved my life, Kid," said Davy weakly. "I thought I was a goner, shore. No, Denver was alone. I think the others were in on it, though, 'cause Denver said he'd helped to kill my uncle."

"I was afraid of that," the Texan muttered. "It means that Tabah is innocent, and that I've helped to put the wrong *hombre* on the scaffold. Listen, Davy. We've got to have a talk. It's pretty cleah now that the men at the ranch . . . some of them, or all . . . ah guilty. But why should they kill yo' uncle?"

"I dunno. I can't think of any grudge they could have had again' him," Davy replied. "Sam was good to everybody . . . too good. And it wasn't robbery, neither."

"Tell me, *amigo,* did Sam Caldwell have any enemies?" suggested Kid. "Anyone who would profit by his death?"

"Not thet I know of, Kid."

"Did he owe any money . . . any business dealin's that yo' know about?" the Texan pressed.

"Well, we had a couple o' dry years. He had to borry a little ready cash," explained the nephew. "Three or four thousand, I think, from Adam Claymore, the banker at Buckhorn. Claymore never seemed anxious about the mortgage, though."

"I should think not. The Box Q is wo'th ten times that," said Kid. "Sometimes, though, a little levah will ovahturn a mighty stone, and maybe that three or fo' thousand was the levah that Claymo' would control. Anyhow, I think I know the answah." Kid Wolf looked thoughtfully at the back trail toward Buckhorn. "In the meantime," he drawled, "in the meantime, Davy. . . ."

"Yes, Kid?"

The Texan's next question mystified Davy. "Do yo' know of any good hide-outs hereabouts . . . a place wheah a man could lay low if need be?"

"Why, yes . . . fer instance, thar's a cave up a cañon of them mountains over yonder." Davy nodded. "I found it once when I was out huntin'. I'll tell you how to get thar. But, Kid, what do you . . . ?"

"You'll know latah, *hombrecito.*" He smiled. "I want yo' to go theah. Yo' certainly can't go to the ranch. Wait theah fo' me. First, though, tell me how to find it."

He listened carefully to Davy's instructions, then he and Davy shook hands and separated, Davy riding toward the mountain retreat, and the Texan starting back in the direction of town.

Davy, looking wonderingly over his shoulder, saw his Texas friend swinging leisurely down the trail, and heard Kid's rich tenor voice raised in song:

Oh, I'd like to be back on the Río Grande, the Río.
Wheah gunsmoke rolls, and bullets wail,
Wheah the lizzahds play on the sand all day,
And the rattlah shakes his ohnery tail.

VIII

Sonny Tabor had been in jail nearly two hours before he recovered consciousness, to find a medico working over him. For a good long time after that, things were very vague and dim.

He was only aware of a pounding headache, and at first he couldn't realize where he was. The last he remembered was the race with the buckskin-clad stranger and the jerk of his rope.

"I'm in jail, no question about that," he muttered as he opened his throbbing eyes and caught a glimpse of steel bars.

He'd lost, then. The buckskin rider and the white horse had been too much for him and Paint. Where was his pinto now? Dead, perhaps. The outlaw was unable to think clearly, and there was a queer buzzing in his ears.

During the afternoon, he began to feel a little better and managed to sit up, resting his bandaged head in his hands. He was the only prisoner in the lockup, but two guards were on duty in the office beyond. It was separated from the cell by a network of iron rods.

"Well, Tabor," said one of the sentries, entering the cell-block, "the killin' of Sam Caldwell was one killin' you didn't get by with. You came to the wrong county, feller."

"What do you mean?"

"You savvy damned well what I mean," jeered the guard. "You wasn't so tough, this time. We got you without losin' a man. You didn't fire a shot."

Sonny felt too sick in mind and body to ask further questions. He didn't know what the man was talking about, but it was plain that another murder, of which he was innocent, had been chalked up against him. That was nothing new to Sonny; it had happened before.

"Would you mind tellin' me what happened to my bronc'?" he managed to ask.

"Kid Wolf took it. He was the man thet got you, so I reckon he's plumb entitled to it," was the reply.

Kid Wolf. So that was the moniker of the man in buck-skins. If it hadn't been for him, Sonny would be free, no doubt, at that moment.

Who was he, anyhow? An officer of some kind? *An Arizona Ranger, maybe,* the outlaw mused. *Well, he done what the reg'lar law couldn't, I'll say that for him.*

He felt no especial bitterness toward Kid Wolf, for Sonny wasn't the sort to bear a grudge. It was tough, though, to be roped like that, and so easily. *I could have killed him, instead of shootin' at his hand,* he thought. *I wonder if Kid Wolf knows that. Oh, well, what's the difference now?*

Supper was brought to him, and he managed to eat a little, although the food tasted like ashes, and the coffee seemed bitter to his palate. He felt stronger, though, after-ward, and soon tottered to the single small window for a look outside.

There was nothing to see—only the ugly backs of some frame buildings. He realized, though, that the town he was in was Buckhorn. The sun had gone, and already the lamps of some of the saloons had been lighted, and he could see the reflection against the darkening sky.

"Do you want me to roll a cigarette fer you?" asked the other guard as Sonny returned to his bunk, with a weary droop to his compact young shoulders.

"*Gracias, amigo*, I don't smoke," said Sonny. "But could I talk to the sheriff, or whoever's in charge of me? I want to ask him about the killin' I'm charged with."

"Sheriff Dougle is in the Hermitage Saloon a-celebratin'," said the sentry. "He prob'ly won't call around ontil tomorrow mornin'. You'd better take it easy. You ain't goin' nowhar, you know," he added with a laugh.

"You're wrong, Simpson," chortled the other guard. "Tabor's goin' on a long, long trip soon, and thar'll be a loop in the end of his ticket."

"Well, he ain't goin' yet a while."

The guards busied themselves in lighting up the two oil lamps that hung from brackets on the walls of the jail office. As they were doing this, someone entered through the street door.

"Good evenin', gentlemen," drawled a voice with a soft Texas accent. "I'd like to see yo' prisonah."

The guards at once became very respectful.

"Well, the sheriff left orders thet we was to let nobody in," said one. "But bein' as you're the man that caught him. . . ."

Sonny Tabor's pulses jumped with interest. He got up and pressed close to the bars, curious to know what kind of man this buckskin rider really was.

As Kid Wolf came striding in, with spurs clanking,

Sonny gave him the once over. Sonny had learned to be a good judge of men, and somehow he liked Kid's looks. He was square, he decided. Dangerous, though, if crossed. That gleam in those steady gray eyes. . . .

"Well, yo' killah, I see they've got you' wheah yo' belong!" Kid cried at sight of the prisoner.

Sonny's heart sank like lead within him. Kid Wolf, too, misjudged him, as did all the others. That hurt. The outlaw had, somehow, admired Kid. But the Texan's next words, spoken in a low tone as he came up to the grated door, were far different, and the outlaw's spirits rocketed once more.

"That was fo' the benefit of yo' guahds," Kid Wolf said softly. "How do yo' feel?"

"Better, thanks." Sonny smiled boyishly.

Kid was silent for a long minute. He seemed to be studying Sonny's face, reading what lay behind Sonny's clear blue eyes. The look was so intense that the outlaw felt uncomfortable.

"Are you a Ranger, Wolf?" he asked.

"No, just a soldah of misfohtune, Sonny," the Texan drawled, "and yo' can call me Kid."

"Well, you've shorely brought some misfortune to me, Kid." The outlaw smiled a bit wistfully. "I can't very well blame you, though. It's quits."

"Not yet," murmured Kid. "Do yo' know anything at all of the murdah of Sam Caldwell . . . the man yo' asked fo' wohk yestahday? I won't ask you to tell the truth. I can tell if yo' lie."

"I don't lie," said Sonny, looking steadily at Kid. "I didn't know the man had been killed. If he has been, I'm sorry, because he treated me white . . . told me to come back and apply at roundup time."

"*Bueno.*" Kid Wolf nodded. "Sonny, what I'm goin' to

do now may seem foolish, but I don't think it is. I'm goin' to get yo' out of heah."

"What?" the outlaw gasped, staring as if he thought the Texan had suddenly lost his mind.

But Kid Wolf had already turned to the guards, who were talking together at the other end of the office.

"Come heah a minute," Kid called to them. "Theah's something the mattah with this cell do'."

They at once pricked up their ears. "Somethin' the matter with the door, is thar? Well, we'll shore have to fix thet. We don't want Tabor a-walkin' out on us."

"What's wrong with the cell door?" demanded the other guard as they hastened up.

"Somethin' very strange. Seems that it won't open," drawled Kid. "Yo'all can fix it," he added slowly, "with the . . . key?"

The guards looked at each other in bewilderment. Kid's next words, snapping like the crack of a blacksnake whip, both horrified and enlightened them.

"Open it! *Pronto!*"

The lower jaws of the guards sagged. A big blued .45 had appeared in each of the Texan's hands. Their yawning black mouths covered them with a dead drop. The guard in charge of the key was so hasty to obey that it fell on the floor three times before he was finally able to control his shaking fingers enough to insert it in the lock. With a harsh creak, the barred door swung ajar.

"All right, Sonny," Kid told the astonished young outlaw. "Let these *hombres* take yo' place."

Sonny came out, staggering a little, more from amazement than weakness, and the two chalky-faced sentries, their knees wobbling under them, entered the cell.

Kid coolly closed the door, locked it carefully, and

tossed the big key into the office spittoon.

"Very sorry to have to treat yo' this way, gentlemen," he said courteously. "Yo'-all won't be heah long, I trust. I would advise, howevah, that yo' refrain from yellin' and hammahin' fo' at least five minutes. Thank yo' kindly."

Leaving the new jailbirds wide-eyed and mute, Kid Wolf and Sonny Tabor slipped into the street.

The outlaw was almost as bewildered as the guards had been. He couldn't realize that he was free.

Kid had chosen an hour when few were on the streets, and fortunately they were not seen, thanks to the twilight that was already deepening into night. The Texan led the way through the nearby side street, where Sonny was overjoyed to see a familiar pony standing at a hitch rail alongside a big white cayuse. It was his own Paint. Not only that, but suspended from the horn of Sonny's saddle were a pair of loaded cartridge belts with two holstered .45s.

"Kid, you've shore made things complete," said the outlaw with a little catch in his voice.

"I'm glad yo' think so." The Texan chuckled. "Now let's sashay out of heah."

Swinging aboard their mounts, the outlaw and the soldier of misfortune swept down the narrow side street and drummed out of town, riding knee to knee. Soon the twinkle of lights was left behind, and they were on the broad, moonlit desert.

Sonny took a deep breath. Freedom again. The soft night air, heavy with the perfume of mesquite and the pleasant aroma of creosote bush, was very sweet.

"Kid, I can't believe it." The outlaw sighed. "I reckon you know my record an' all. Paint and me . . . well, we're thankin' you a lot. It's all we can say, but I guess you savvy how we feel."

"It's all right, Sonny *amigo*," the Texan drawled. "Bein' as I got yo' into the jam, I figgahed it was up to me to get yo' out. Besides, I've somethin' to tell yo'."

He told the interested outlaw of San Caldwell's death, of affairs at the Box Q, and of Davy's trouble. It was a mess, as he said, and a puzzle, although he was beginning to glimpse the light of day.

It was close to midnight before they reached the hidden cañon. An attempt would be made to track them, of course, and they were careful to leave as baffling a trail as possible. The cave was found without difficulty, for after climbing for some distance up the narrow cañon they made out a ruddy glow against the cliffs.

Davy had made a little fire and had everything snug and shipshape. He was round-eyed at the sight of Kid Wolf's companion. He jumped as if a bee had stung him.

"Davy." Kid chuckled. "I want yo' to shake hands with mah guest . . . mah friend, Sonny Tabah."

IX

The three friends passed all that day and all of the next quietly in the hiding place Davy had found for them. The Texan had provided plenty of provisions, and there was a spring nearby, so they were comfortable enough.

On the first day, Kid climbed to a high vantage point from which he could view the surrounding country, and he saw the dust of several posses. Sheriff Dougle was scouring the country, but in vain.

The Texan and Sonny Tabor became well acquainted during those two days of careful waiting. The outlaw told of some of his escapades and narrow squeaks of the past, and in turn the Texan recounted some of his own adventures. Davy listened to them both, wide-eyed and open-mouthed. He had been a bit afraid of Sonny at first, but nobody could be with the outlaw long without liking and understanding him, and soon Davy was admiring him as much as Kid.

As the second afternoon wore to a close, the Texan's eyes met Sonny Tabor's. Both of them had the same thought. It was high time to be doing things.

"I reckon the search has petered out by now," Sonny said, the bullet-scar dimple on his brown cheek deepening as he smiled.

"Yes, I think it's time we made ouah little call on the Box Q *caballeros*," Kid drawled. "Fo' Davy's sake, it's time we reached a soht of undahstandin' with them. It's his ranch, and it's time they were vacatin'. It will be up to them as to just how they'll vacate."

"Kin I go along, too, Kid?" asked Davy eagerly.

"I'm afraid it won't be safe fo' yo'," decided the Texan. "I'll tell yo' what . . . yo' wait heah for an houh aftah we're gone. Then ride cautious-like to the ranch. If yo' see a lamp buhnin' in the south window, yo'll know it's all right. Othahwise . . . well, yo' had bettah go to town fo' the sheriff."

Davy's lips trembled a little, but he nodded. He realized what would probably happen at the Box Q.

"If I'm any judge of men, they won't be doin' any wohk," said Kid as he rolled a brown cigarette. "If we strike the ranch house right aftah dahk, I'm sho' we'll find them theah, unless they happen to be in town."

At sundown, Sonny and Kid swung aboard their broncos. It promised to be a quiet, cloudless night, and a rind of silver moon was already shining in the east.

"Remembah, Davy," said the Texan gravely, "wait at

least an houah befo' yo' follow us, and then don't come neah the house unless yo' see ouah signal."

"All right," Davy faltered. "Take keer of yourselves. Thar's four of them snakes, countin' the Chinaman, an' they're plenty good with guns."

"I'm glad to heah it," drawled the Texan dryly. "That will make it mo' interestin'."

"Don't worry, Davy," Sonny said, reaching down from his saddle to squeeze the youngster's hand. "We'll straighten things out fer you."

Kid Wolf and the outlaw drummed rapidly away through the deepening twilight. It was only seven or eight miles to the Box Q headquarters.

Pleased to friskiness at being in the open country again, Blizzard and Paint kicked up their heels gaily and nickered at each other. Like their masters, they seemed to get along well together.

"I think Paint could take Blizzard's measuah ovah rough country," drawled Kid. "Next to Blizzahd, yo' pinto is the best cayuse I know about, Sonny."

"Well, your hoss is the best *caballo* I've ever seen . . . next to Paint." Sonny laughed.

They rounded another spur of the mountains, crossed a mesquite-dotted plain, and then found themselves within sight of their objective. A half mile ahead, under the gloom of tall cottonwood trees, they saw the black oblong of the ranch house. Yellow lamplight gleamed from the windows.

"There's somebody, anyway," Sonny muttered.

They dismounted a good distance from the house, leaving their horses standing in the shadow of the corral. Then they went forward on foot, the deep sand deadening even the tinkle of their spurs.

Kid signaled to Sonny to approach one of the side windows. It might be a good idea to see and hear what they could before going in. The blind was partly drawn, but they got a good view of the interior, and, as the sash was raised an inch or so, they could hear perfectly.

The traitorous foreman, the bleary-eyed Fred Graffman, and the Apache wrangler, Injun Frank, were in the room. Ling Foo was not in evidence, although they could hear him moving around to the clatter of pots and pans in the kitchen beyond.

"I cain't savvy it," Hogar was saying. "Not a-tall, I don't."

"It did give me a jar when I went to the bottom of the bluff this mornin' and found Denver layin' thar shot to death," growled Graffman, who was more than half drunk.

Several jugs and bottles stood on the littered table, along with cigarette stubs, soiled glasses, and decks of cards. The gang had certainly taken over the Box Q, for the time, at least.

"Who do you reckon did it? Do you reckon thet Tabor . . . ?"

"No, from the news I got Tabor didn't break jail ontil that evenin'," Graffman said. "Denver was shore kilt not long after we'd left him."

"What gits me," Hogar muttered uneasily, "is whar's Davy? We'd better sober up, and go into town tomorrow. We'll have a talk with Claymore, anyhow."

Hogar and Graffman were pacing the floor nervously.

Injun Frank, as wooden-faced as ever, sat at the end of the table, smoking a corn-husk cigarette.

"It was a funny thing," Graffman snorted, "Wolf helpin' Tabor out o' the *calabozo*. What did he do it fer? And if he kilt Denver, why did he do it? Now thet Tabor's loose, I don't know what to think. I don't feel easy in my mind.

Suppose Tabor had heard somethin' . . . suppose he came *here*."

"Afraid?" sneered Hogar, loosening the Colt in his holster and squaring his shoulders. "Well, I'm not, nor of thet Texas Wolf, either. I'd like to git a chance at 'em. Wolf caught me off balance the other day, or I'd have sent him a-howlin' up the flume."

Graffman poured a glass brimful of whiskey, carried it to his thick lips with a shaky hand, and drank it at a gulp. "Sometimes I wish I hadn't got in on this scheme in the fust place," he mumbled.

"Yeah?" sneered Hogar. "You kin use the *dinero,* all right, can't you? And even if we don't collect the extry thousand for puttin' the *muchacho* out o' the way, we've still got five comin' from Claymore fer killin' old Sam. He'll pay, too, and, if he balks. . . ."

Kid Wolf and Sonny drew away from the window. They had heard enough. Exchanging a quick hand clasp, they noiselessly rounded the corner of the house.

"Do you reckon the door's locked, Kid?" the outlaw breathed.

"We won't take chances of warnin' 'em by rattlin' the knob, if it is," Kid decided. "Heah we ah. We'll rain it in. When I say three, we'll hit it with ouah boots. Aftah that . . . well, I guess I don't need to tell yo' what to do." He smiled grimly. "One . . . two . . . three!"

With a sudden rending, splintering crash, the door flew from its hinges and banged to the floor of the room.

"Good evenin', *caballeros,*" the Texan drawled.

X

If the earth had unexpectedly opened and emitted two demons, Hogar and his partners couldn't have been more astounded. Graffman gave a screech of fear. The foreman's drink-blotched face whitened, and even Injun Frank jumped to his feet with a wheezing intake of breath. For just the fraction of a moment, the desperadoes and their uninvited visitors faced one another. Then things began to happen.

"Wolf . . . and Tabor!" Hogar yelped. "Drop 'em . . . quick!"

His hand streaked from left to right in a deadly, fast cross-body draw. At the same moment, Graffman and Injun Frank jerked at their holstered guns.

Until that moment, Sonny's and Kid's hands were empty. They didn't stay that way long. Kid and the outlaw jumped apart, landing, spraddled on the toes of their boots. Flame and smoke belched forth from the level, almost, of their knees.

The Box Q traitors were shooting, too. The room instantly became a smoking furnace of gunfire. A blue haze dimmed the lamp, and the flashes of heavy Colts winked through the curtain of powder fog. The house seemed to shudder; the very ground seemed to shake and vibrate.

"Have mercy!" shrieked Graffman, but he was already dying. Clawing at his chest where two of the Texan's bullets had smashed him, he slumped to the floor, coughing.

Injun Frank, too, had been hit, but he clutched the table edge to steady himself, and kept shooting. His face was not so expressionless now. The agonized fear of the hereafter had dawned into his evil black eyes. Already a dark stain

213

was expanding over the shoulder of his dirty shirt. He was swaying, reeling.

The thunder of guns was like the beating of hammers on the anvil of death. Hogar had thrown himself backward, against the wall, and was trying desperately to kill. But Sonny Tabor and Kid, wreathed in smoke of their own making, were hard to hit. They bobbed and shifted—and dealt lead.

A slug had sliced Kid's sombrero from his head. Another had scorched Sonny's neck, but their guns kept going.

"Blame your crimes on me, will you?" Sonny shouted over the noise.

He sent another .45 slug into Injun Frank, the finish shot for the Apache. With his murderous heart stilled forever, the coppery killer thudded to the floor, his gun still smoking in his stiffening fingers.

Sonny and Kid shot Hoke Hogar at the same instant. The awful roar of guns ended abruptly, and there was a silence so intense that it hurt. The stillness was broken by a hideous scream from Hogar. The foreman had dropped his gun, but he still leaned, dying, against the wall. One bullet had hit him below the breastbone, another had struck his face, and his jaw was hanging loosely, dangling queerly. Crimson was splashed on the plaster all around him. He made a last effort and hurled the lamp at Kid. Then he fell. The lamp smashed, went out, and the room was plunged into darkness. The Texan had dodged it just in time.

Then a wide band of yellow light cut the blackness of the smoky room. The kitchen door had been opened. The poisonous face of Ling Foo was framed in the light.

Kid ducked low. Something had zipped over his head, and he heard a deadly *thud* in the wall behind him. The Chinaman had hurled a knife. He was reaching into the

wide sleeve of his jacket, preparing to throw another. Kid
could have shot him, but, instead, his right hand darted behind his ear. It reappeared with a big Texas Bowie knife.

"Yo' have chosen the weapon, sah!" crackled Kid's
voice.

Kid Wolf always carried that knife, in a hidden sheath
sewed inside the collar of his buckskin shirt, for a hole card.
He hurled it now with the same grace of motion as his draw.
There was a twanging noise, then a little sigh from Ling
Foo who quietly folded up into a huddled heap. The big
Bowie knife had buried itself to the hilt in his throat. He'd
been beaten at his own game.

Making sure that spidery Ling Foo was finished, Kid
stepped over him and went into the kitchen for the other
lamp.

"I reckon we can signal to Davy now, Sonny," he said as
he put the light in the south window.

Kid Wolf, Sonny Tabor, and young Davy did not linger
long on the Box Q. It was not a very cheerful place now.

"We can't very well leave yo' heah, Davy, and we have
some business to attend to in town," suggested Kid. "Have
yo' any friends neahby that yo' could go to?"

"I know the folks at the AC Connected," Davy said.
"They'd be glad to take me in. They was good friends of my
uncle's. Thet ranch is right on the way to Buckhorn."

"*Bueno,*" said Kid. "We'll see yo' safely theah."

At the side road that led to the ranch house of Davy's
friends, they took leave of him. He understood Sonny and
the Texan well enough now not to try to thank them for
what they had done, or were about to do. But he had to
blink back the tears when they bade him good bye.

"Will I see you again someday?" he faltered.

"*¿Quién sabe?* We hope so." The outlaw smiled. "Anyway, Kid and me are goin' to make the Box Q a safe place fer you. It's yours, *amigo,* and we're ridin' into town to make shore it stays yours."

"I'll never forgit what you've done," said Davy, manfully blinking back his emotion. "*Adiós,* pards!"

Kid and the outlaw rode on through the desert toward Buckhorn. For a long time, they were silent, each busy with his own thoughts.

"I hated to have to kill those sidewinders back at the Box Q," Sonny said finally.

"It was them, or us and Davy, too," Kid reminded him. "But like yo', Sonny, I regret the necessity fo' it. I was just thinking, *compadre* . . . yo' mustn't go into town with me. It would be too dangerous fo' yo'."

"I'll take the chance." The outlaw smiled. "What we have to do shouldn't take long. I'm seein' it through with you, Kid."

It was past midnight when they reached Buckhorn. Save for the brilliantly lighted saloons, the streets were dark, and all was quiet and serene. Whistling softly his favorite tune, the Texan led the way toward a small building at the lower end of the town. He'd remembered seeing a sign over it that read:

ADAM CLAYMORE
Private Banker—Loans—Lands

XI

Claymore lived in a couple of rooms behind the large one that faced the street and served as his office. He was a light sleeper, and, when the knock sounded on his window, he was quick to get out of bed.

"Who's that?" he called out as he slipped his trousers over his nightshirt.

"Customers," was the reply.

"Jist a minute, and I'll light the lamp, and let you in the front way," Claymore sang back eagerly.

Like most sharks who do a shady business, Adam Claymore kept very irregular office hours, and to be called from his sleep was nothing very unusual. He was miserly enough not to want to lose a dollar, honest or otherwise, that he could get his greedy fingers on. Applying a match to the wick of a kerosene lamp, he hastened with it to his business office, fumbling for his keys.

Claymore's headquarters were peculiar, looking more like a pack rat's nest than a place where lands and money changed hands. There was a big safe in one corner, with Adam Claymore's name in faded gilt, and letter files as high as the ceiling were stacked against the gloomy walls. Papers were strewn over the floor and thick dust was on everything. His desk and chair were in the center of the room, piled high with odds and ends, pens, and inkwells.

"I hope your business is important," he said as he unlocked the door. "At this hour. . . ."

"It's very important," the reply came, and the banker swung the door open with a satisfied chuckle that instantly changed to a squeak of alarm. He tried to slam it again, but a tall man in fringed buckskins had calmly put his foot in the opening. "Wolf . . . and . . . and . . . Sonny Tabor," Claymore gasped, backing slowly into the room as his visitors walked coolly in. "What . . . what . . . ?"

"Take a chaih, sah," said the Texan sternly.

Claymore's long, thin face had turned a greenish yellow.

Why hadn't he buckled on his six-gun? What chance, though, would he have against Kid Wolf and the worst outlaw in the Southwest? The banker seemed about to be sick at the stomach. "I . . . I won't open the safe," he piped weakly.

"We ah not heah to rob yo'," said Kid contemptuously. "Sit down theah. We want to talk to yo'."

Adam Claymore fell rather than sat in his desk chair, and Kid Wolf calmly drew up one opposite. Sonny remained standing beside the desk, watching the banker's every move.

"What do you want with me?" demanded Claymore, his voice weak and trembling.

"We've just come from the Box Q, sah," the Texan drawled carelessly, one leg over the other and rolling a cigarette with leisurely fingers. "No use beatin' around the bush, Claymo'. Sonny and I know everything."

The banker opened his blue lips to speak, but no sound came. A great terror was in his little eyes.

"We know," continued the Texan relentlessly, "that yo' had Hogar and his men kill Sam Caldwell. Yo' hiahed 'em to do it. Yo' wanted Davy killed, too, but that scheme didn't wohk . . . fohtunately. Yo'ah a murdahah. Hogar and his pahds have paid the price, and so must yo'."

"I . . . I didn't. . . ." Claymore met the cold gray eyes of Kid Wolf and the icy blue ones of Sonny Tabor, and the denial died away in his throat.

"Yo' have a mohtgage, or notes against the Box Q," hinted the Texan. "Yo' cain't buy off justice, sah, but it will go easiah with yo' if yo' hand them ovah. Ah they in the safe yondah?"

"In . . . in my desk here," quavered the banker. He took a key from his trousers pocket, inserted it into the lock with trembling fingers, and pulled it open. "I'll . . . do as you say," he gasped.

As he reached into the drawer, a desperate resolve was born to him. Adam Claymore was a coward, but he was cornered now, trapped. His groping fingers had touched the chill metal of the gun he always kept there—a blunt little .41 Derringer, double-barreled. He could take the Texan with him to death, at least, and with a little luck. . . . "You've got me all wrong," he said, licking his thin lips nervously. "If the Box Q bunch said I'd hired 'em to do any killin's, they lied." He was stalling for time now, his forefinger was searching out the trigger. He wouldn't even have to draw out the .41. A quick shot through the desk. . . . "Sam was a friend o' mine," he whined. "I wouldn't kill him. He was a great friend, Sam was."

"I hope I'm never blessed with such friends," said Kid grimly. "Yo' hurry, sah, and find. . . ."

The room was suddenly and violently shaken by an explosion—several of them, rather, but blended so closely together that they sounded like one. Kid sprang from his chair, astonished to see a blued six-gun in Sonny Tabor's hand, emitting curls of thin blue smoke. More smoke was coming from the drawer of the banker's desk. Adam Claymore was huddled down in his chair, his head to one side. He'd been shot through the temples.

"I beat him to it," said the outlaw slowly. "Are you hurt, Kid?"

"Never touched me," the Texan gasped. "Yo' sho' saved my life by spoilin' his aim that way. I'm bettin' that bullet didn't miss me by mo' than six inches, as it was. I was cahless . . . should have been mo' watchful."

Flames were shooting up from the mass of papers in the drawer now. The exploding Derringer had set alight a box of matches. Sonny yanked it fully open and began slapping at the fire with his Stetson, soon putting it out.

"Look, Kid. Here's what we want," he said quickly as he picked a half-charred document from the remains. "It's signed Sam Caldwell. I'll finish burnin' it," and, striking a match, he put the end of the Box Q's treacherous debt.

"*Bueno,* Sonny. Let's ride, *pronto,* befo' the whole town's swahmin' around us."

They sprinted for the street, and not a bit too soon, either. For the shots had been heard, and men were running from the nearest saloons. Before Buckhorn could quite realize what had happened, however, and who had visited it, two cayuses, a white one and a pinto, were storming out of town. For a mile they galloped, then slowed and took things more easily, breathing in the crisp air of the glorious Arizona night. All was still, except for the call of lonely coyotes and the faint rustlings of the mesquites. On all sides, somber mountain ranges loomed, ghost-like under the blinking stars.

Sonny finally drew his pinto to a halt. "I've been dreadin' this, but I'm afraid it's got to be *adiós* now, *amigo,*" he said in a low voice. "Our trails had better divide here. I'm an outlaw, you know, a condemned fugitive. I don't want to get you into trouble."

"I'm already an outlaw mahself as fah as Buckhohn County is concerned," Kid muttered. "Listen, Sonny. The West is wide. Come with me. Leave yo' reputation, yo' name behind yo'. With anothah name, in anothah paht of the country. . . ."

"Thanks, Kid," replied the outlaw slowly, "but I couldn't do that. I'm not ashamed of my name, or of anything I've done. Arizona's my own country, and I've got to clear my record here before I go anywhere else. Someday, maybe. . . ."

"But theah's a death sentence hangin' ovah yo', Sonny," Kid protested. "Yo'ah wanted, dead or alive."

"I'm not afraid," said Sonny Tabor quietly. He ran his hand through Paint's silky mane and smiled. "Me and Paint will see it through . . . to the end. Good bye, Kid. We'll never forget you."

"I think I undahstand, pardnah."

They exchanged a quick, hard hand clasp, then abruptly turned their horses in opposite directions, as if they were afraid of betraying their emotions. Their trail had forked. The buckskin-clad Texan rode northward, Sonny toward the south. The rhythmic throb of hoofs faded, died away into silence at last, and a pink blush in the east announced a new sunrise over Arizona.

About the Author

Paul Sylvester Powers was a prolific and well-known pulp Western writer whose characters enraptured an entire generation of *Wild West Weekly* readers during the Great Depression. He was born in 1905 in Little River, Kansas. Despite the wishes of his father—the town doctor—he spurned a career in medicine and decided to try his hand at writing fiction. In 1928 he sold his first story, "The Whispering Gunman", to *Wild West Weekly*, which began a fifteen-year run with the magazine. Sonny Tabor, Kid Wolf and Freckles Malone were written under the pseudonym Ward M. Stevens. Johnny Forty-Five was written under the *Wild West Weekly* house name (meaning it was shared by other writers) of Andrew Griffin. Besides these characters, he also created King Kolt, the Fightin Three of the Rockin T, and wrote countless short stories for *Wild West Weekly*, all of which were written under his own name. Altogether he wrote 430 stories for *Wild West Weekly*. After the magazine folded in 1943, he continued to write for *Western Story*, *Thrilling Ranch Stories*, *Texas Rangers*, *West*, and *Thrilling Western*. *Wolf of the Rio Grande* will be his next Five Star Western.

About the Editor

Laurie Powers grew up in Livermore, California, and the foothills of the Sierra Nevada. She has been an escrow officer in Beverly Hills, a scuba diving instructor, and in 1997 she entered Smith College. Her honors thesis, "On the Trail of Sonny Tabor: True Confessions of a Pulp Writer's Granddaughter", was awarded Highest Honors in American Studies. Laurie is now a technical editor and writer in northern California. She has continued to research pulp fiction and works with her grandfather's children in assembling one of the largest private collections of *Wild West Weekly* issues in the country.